DEADLY DIAMOND

(A Murfy the Cat Mystery)

by

Anna Kern

Copyright 2015 by Anna Kern

For information, email **Cozy Cat Press**, cozycatpress@aol.com or visit our website at: www.cozycatpress.com

COZY CAT
P R E S S

ISBN: 978-1-939816-66-5

Printed in the United States of America

Cover design by Paula Ellenberger
http://www.paulaellenberger.com/

1 2 3 4 5 6 7 8 9 10

Dedicated to the memory of Pooky
January 1, 2015

I put down my book, The Meaning of Zen, *and see the cat smiling into her fur as she delicately combs it with her rough pink tongue. "Cat, I would lend you this book to study but it appears you have already read it." She looks up and gives me her full gaze. "Don't be ridiculous," she purrs, "I wrote it."*
—From *Miao* by Dily Laing

Beachside, Florida, December 15:

    Friday morning, ten days before Christmas, shoppers crowded the sidewalks in downtown Beachside, a tourist town on the east coast of Florida still in the process of renovation, the physical location not beach side, as the name implies, but about two miles inland.

    Christmas decorations were up—huge wreaths and banners hanging from the art-deco style streetlights, and tiny lights wrapped around palm trees planted at equal intervals on the brick sidewalk. Some of the storefronts of the mostly art-deco style buildings decked according to the owner's personal taste were not at all in keeping with the classy image the city wanted to portray. Tourists and locals in shorts and sandals were in the holiday spirit even though the temperature was in the eighties—not bothered by the incongruity of the frosted glass windows and the hot sun scorching their skin.

    A slight-built man of average looks lingered near the entrance of Hall's Jewelry. His pale complexion and white legs pegged him as a tourist of an undetermined age. He took a quick look up and down the street, and wiped the palms of his hands on his gray, cargo shorts before he entered.

The store was busier than usual, and that was a plus. Nevertheless, he looked a little disconcerted when he walked in and saw the security guard as none of the merchants on Ocean Street had ever hired a security guard before. His upper lip twitched—the security guard was unexpected, but the guard was old and slow; he could outrun him if necessary. He squared his shoulders, meandered to the counter displaying diamond engagement rings and waited for the wide-eyed, sales associate behind the counter to finish up with her customer.

After looking at several rings and not liking any of them, he said, "My girl is amazing ... I want the ring to be exceptional...." He gave her a half-smile. "Do you have some loose diamonds you could show me? I have an idea for the setting, and perhaps that would be the best way to go."

Vainly running her fingers through a mop of copper red hair, and avoiding eye contact with the other customers waiting for her assistance, she put away the last two rings he'd asked to see.

"As you probably know, we deal mostly in estate jewelry, so we don't really have a large selection of loose diamonds."

"Yes, I know that," he said, perhaps a bit too sharply. "What you do have will be unique, I'm sure," he added with a disarming smile.

"Please step down to the end of the counter," and to the other customers, she said, "I'll be with you as soon as I can."

Although, there was nothing to be suspicious about, she located the security guard before she unlocked the bottom drawer of the glass case. She took out a tray and set it on the counter.

"We have a beautiful marquee cut, two-carat, retails at fifteen thousand," she said as she handed him an eye loupe.

"Um...I think I'd like a traditional round stone," and he returned the diamond to her. He selected another from the tray, pretended to drop it accidently, and replaced it with the glass one he had in his hand.

He made it a point of looking at his watch. "Hey, I didn't realize it was so late. My girlfriend is in the shoe store down the street, and she's going to come looking for me any minute if she doesn't see me out there waiting for her," he said, edging away from the counter.

"Do you live here or are you a visitor?"

"Yeah," he said, his eyes darting about, "I live here. I'm going to have to come back another time, though. Thanks a lot for your help."

The diamond safely in his hand, he hurried toward the exit, and paused long enough to look back and see the sales associate reach for the eye loupe.

"Since each of us is blessed with only one life, why not live it with a cat?"
—Robert Stearns

CHAPTER ONE: *Misty's Indignation*

Friday morning, ten days before Christmas, Misty and I were on duty at Antiques & Designs. I was at my post on the checkout counter keeping a watchful eye on things while Misty, a smallish cat with a quirky personality, viewed the parade of humans passing by the display window.

Alyx Hille and her best friend Maggie Broeck are the owners of the store. Alyx, five feet two inches tall, brown hair cut in a shaggy sort of style, hazel eyes and a beautiful smile, generously shares her home with Misty, Pooky—who prefers the security of home—and me. My name is Murfy and I'm also a Felis catus. I look and behave like an ordinary cream tabby with green eyes, but I'm not—ordinary, that is. Alyx is my human, and my mission is to comfort and protect her, no matter what it takes.

Althea Burns, a frail, older woman, made her last payment on the late eighteenth-century George III, slant-front desk that Alyx had been holding for her, and asked what time to expect delivery.

"It will be sometime this afternoon for sure. I'll give you a call later about the exact time. Okay?"

"All right, Alyx, I'll wait to hear from you."

As Althea walked past me, she said she wished she could find a playmate for her cat. She'd voiced that thought before. Fortunately, Alyx had never acted on Althea's request and, I must admit, I was a little disappointed when she agreed today.

"How about I bring Murfy with me and introduce him to your cat when we deliver your desk?"

"That would be wonderful, Alyx! I'll see you and Murfy later."

As Althea walked out, a slight built man entered the store. He pulled his black baseball cap lower over his wrap-around sunglasses and in the process bumped into Althea, saying nothing in the way of an apology. He wiped his hands on his shorts, and quickly made his way directly to the slant-front desk scheduled for delivery that afternoon.

Sitting next to the store's only concession to the season—red candles in an elaborate antique candelabrum surrounded by a Holly branch—Misty observed the man intently.

The commotion caused by a screaming child being dragged out of the store momentarily diverted my attention, and when I looked back, the man was running his hand over the inlaid work on the desk, keeping his eyes averted, refusing to make eye contact with anyone.

A couple of minutes later, he turned to leave and tripped over Misty, her indignation heard all over the store. I bounced off the counter and ran to her aid ready to do battle if necessary.

Now, all eyes were on the man. Alyx started to say, "I'm so sorry …"

The man lowered his head, sidestepped over me, and ignored her as he hastened past.

Bernice, one of the store employees, came up to the counter and asked Alyx, "What was that all about?"

"That was the strangest thing—I don't know what it was all about. I'd better go check on Misty, and make sure she's all right."

Misty, a gray cat with blue eyes, wasn't used to rough treatment, and getting stepped on hurt her feelings—put her out of sorts, and she sought refuge under a highboy. No amount of cajoling could get her to come out, so Alyx let her be. I figured she'd have to come out eventually, so I sat nearby and offered moral support.

Alyx left and returned a short time later carrying the design board and samples she'd worked on that morning. She dropped it all on the counter when Maggie Broeck flew through the front door, slightly out of breath, her face flushed.

"Alyx, you're not going to believe what just happened; Hall's Jewelry was robbed!"

"You were there in the store?"

"Yes, I walked in right after it happened."

Alyx pulled up a chair for Maggie and one for herself.

"As we discussed yesterday, I went to see Chet Hall about next month's Downtown Merchants Association meeting. The police arrived right after I walked in, and I stayed to find out what happened. I heard Susan say that someone stole a thirty thousand dollar loose diamond. She said she got suspicious when the customer left abruptly. She examined the last diamond that he'd looked at and discovered it was glass. The security guard ran after the thief, but lost him in the crowd."

"I didn't think Chet traded in such expensive stones."

Maggie shrugged her shoulders. "I guess he doesn't usually; this was a special case. He wanted to help out a longtime resident, a widow in financial need due to her husband's medical bills."

"I guess it was only a matter of time before thieves found their way downtown," Alyx stated with an obvious note of disillusionment as she glanced at the antique train station clock on the wall.

"Maggie, I have to leave right now if I don't want to give our new client a reason to fire me. I should be back in about an hour. If you speak to George in the meantime, ask him what time he can deliver Althea's desk."

Alyx was back from her meeting with the new client when George called about an hour later. Maggie answered and smiled into the receiver. The conversation was short.

"George said he can deliver the desk at four."

"That's perfect," said Alyx. "Althea was here earlier, and she's very excited about finally getting the desk home. As much as I hate to see that desk leave the store, I'm glad it's going to Althea. It has more meaning for her than it does for me."

Maggie was noticeably quiet.

"Is everything okay with you and George?"

"Yes, everything is fine. What makes you think something's wrong?"

"Based on your cryptic comments in the last couple of weeks, I sense that something is going on underneath the surface."

"I know you don't think he's my type because he's average-looking and shy, and it surprised me too when I started seeing him. George is a kind, gentle man. There's nothing going on, and I don't want to talk about it now anyway."

Alyx closed the catalog in front of her, placed it back on the shelf with the others, and casually changed the subject by asking, "Do you mind if I take off a little early today?"

"Of course not. Are you nervous about tonight?"

"No, I'm not at all. I guess the fact that I've seen David and spoken to him often during the past few months makes it seem normal to have dinner with him. I'm looking forward to a pleasant evening with a sexy, handsome man. I hope I don't act too eager and scare him away."

"What? You act too eager or David get scared? Neither one is a remote possibility."

"I'm not sure how to take that, so I'll ignore it and keep you out of trouble."

"I hope your cats like your choice of dress this time," Maggie said with a smile, referring to a panicked call she'd received the night of a dinner party that Alyx had hosted earlier that year.

"I'd keep my clothes away from the cats, if I were you; they're not only smart, they have good taste," Maggie teased.

"One is never sure, watching two cats washing each other, whether it's affection, the taste or a trial run for the jugular."
—Helen Thomson

CHAPTER TWO: *Hidden Treasure*

Misty was always ready to play a game of hide-and-seek, and I searched for her where I last left her. The game was a simple one, and served its purpose; I hid, waited for her to walk by, and pounced on her. Sometimes the playing did get a little out of hand and my nip turned into a bite, forcing her to defend herself. Misty doesn't hold grudges; and the bite was soon forgotten, although the self-defense lesson was not.

I spied her sitting next to the desk that the nervous man had been examining when he stepped on her. When she spotted me heading her way, she took off at a gallop, under, over and around the antiques and vintage furniture, looking over her shoulder to make sure I followed. I caught up with her on the wide, majestic staircase off to the side of the room, curving up to the loft area on the second floor. I was mystified, as this was a very different Misty.

She led the way to the back section of the loft that was closed to customers, and filled with broken furniture that handyman George Lucas would one-day repair or recycle into something else. I nimbly jumped on a three-legged table supported by another piece of furniture. It took Misty two false starts before she made it to the top.

What she had to say was troubling; the man who'd stepped on her wasn't wearing sunglasses or a cap when he'd walked by the display window, she said. He'd pulled them from his pockets and put them on right before he walked into the store.

To my knowledge, humans have poor vision and generally take off their sunglasses when they go indoors, so why go to the trouble of disguising himself before entering the store?

Misty lifted her back leg, licked it a couple of times and left it up in the air, distracted by I don't know what. I licked her ear to get her refocused on her story, and she continued.

Apparently, when the man was examining the desk, he opened some of the small drawers, took whatever he was chewing out of his mouth, and stuck it in one of the drawers. She said she went to take a closer look and that's when the brute stepped on her.

Contrary to popular belief, cats can process information as quickly as any human can. It was obvious that the man was trying to disguise himself, and if my deduction was correct, the man who stepped on Misty was the diamond thief.

The problem was how to relay the information to Alyx. Communication with those of my kind has never been difficult. We have our ways. Humans use words, and that's the problem. Misty, however, was sure I'd figure something out—I always did.

I complimented her on a job well done. She said she needed a snack, jumped from the table, hit the floor with her chin, and walked away as if that was the only way to land. She pranced down the stairs, and I followed her to the checkout counter where she fished out her favorite bag of soft treats from the basket that customers kept full. The classy, raven-haired woman tapping her manicured fingers on the counter paid no attention, and with the bag awkwardly dangling from her mouth, Misty walked away in search of someone to open it for her.

The woman at the counter didn't wait long before she left, and I turned my attention back to the slant-front desk. I stood on my hind legs, peered in the pigeonholes that flanked a central-banded door and tried to open the variety of small drawers. The experience tired me out. I then drifted back upstairs for a nap, and, disturbed by what Misty had told me, I didn't fall asleep right away.

You see, I left home at a very young age and my mother didn't have time to teach me much of anything. I do remember her telling me that according to legend, I had the mark of the gods—the *M* on my forehead was proof of it. Supposedly, that mark made me special. I don't think it's only because of the mark—I do have a brain—and it was telling me that the thief hid the diamond in the desk.

*"Everything I know I learned from my cat. When you're
hungry, eat. When you're tired, nap in a sunbeam.
When you go to the vet's, pee on your owner."*
—Gary Smith

CHAPTER THREE: *Murfy Goes on a Playdate*

George arrived promptly at four that afternoon and
unloaded his latest project; an old dresser converted
into a dining room buffet. He chatted with Maggie
while Alyx wrapped up what she was working on, and
we were all ready to go a few minutes later. Alyx told
George that she would take her own car as she planned
to stay and visit for a while. She wrote the address on a
slip of paper and handed it to him.

"Do you know where it is?" she asked.

"I know exactly where it is. You want to follow
me?"

"Sure," she said, "I'll get Murfy while you load the
desk, unless you need help."

He winked at Maggie and flexed his arm. "Nothing I
can't handle. Right, Maggie?" She smiled indulgently
and followed him.

Aware of what Alyx expected me to do, I reluctantly
stepped into the carrier. I really wasn't looking forward
to meeting this Simon cat. I considered hiding, knowing
they'd never find me until I was ready to be found.
Although I certainly didn't need a playmate as I had
two felines at home, apparently Simon did. Looking on
the bright side, I could play a little rougher with him

than with the females at home. A real wrestling match might be fun.

At Althea's condominium, Alyx left me in the carrier while George unloaded the desk. The designer in Alyx must have been dismayed to see so many rooms cramped with furniture. Althea told Alyx that she'd downsized through the years, but it didn't look like it to me.

Once George settled the desk in its new location in the study, Althea asked if they had time for some refreshments.

"Something cold would be great," answered George, wiping his brow with his t-shirt.

"I have some scones, and I made iced tea. Alyx, would you like hot tea instead?"

The teapot was already sitting on a silver tray, along with some pretty cups. Alyx said she'd love some.

Alyx let me out of the carrier and I followed her and George to the small kitchen where Althea had set the table for afternoon tea. I freely explored the area, helping myself to a snack from Simon's food bowl, followed by a drink from his bowl of fresh water.

Althea poured a glass of iced tea for George and asked him if making furniture was a hobby or a business.

"It's both. I had a small shop in Vermont where I built furniture pieces by special order; now I do it as a hobby."

"From what I've seen in the store, you do beautiful work. You're too young for retirement, what made you decide to quit?"

George crossed and uncrossed his legs. "It's a long story, so let's just say mostly because of divorce and all the financial problems that come with it."

Alyx then steered the conversation back to small talk and when he left, I finally got to met Simon.

"Okay, Althea," said Alyx, "let's introduce our fur-babies and see how that goes."

"All right, dear; should I go get Simon?"

Alyx hooked the leash to my collar. "No, not yet. I'm going to bring Murfy to him. You don't think he'll attack, do you?"

I knew her concern was more for the other cat getting hurt than for me. Regardless, I was glad to hear Althea say that she didn't think so.

"He's always acted quite the gentleman around other animals in the vet's waiting room."

I couldn't help the shiver that ruffled my fur at the mention of that word. Surely, there's no domestic animal alive, no matter how tough, that doesn't fear the dreaded *V* word.

"Well, he's not tied up, so he has the option to run away if he wants to."

Althea opened the laundry room door, and Simon sauntered out. Detecting neither fear nor aggression, Simon, a pleasant enough fellow, moved away to hunch down on all fours, studying me, while I sat politely, studying him.

Both Alyx and Althea were smiling at the successful encounter. "I think they need to get acquainted."

Althea asked Alyx if she wanted another cup of tea. Alyx said yes, went down on one knee, and unhooked my leash.

Simon bounded away, looking behind his left shoulder, inviting me to follow him, which I did, but stayed close enough to hear the conversation between the two women.

"Alyx, I'd like to hire you to help me redecorate this room; I know I have far too many things in here. I saw it on your face that you agree."

"I can see why you kept them. They are truly outstanding pieces. If you'd like, I can take what you don't want to keep and sell them for you," she suggested.

"You mean on consignment?"

"Yes, exactly."

The ever-present vulnerability on Althea's face momentarily disappeared. "What would your percentage be?"

Alyx stammered a reply, "We don't … as a rule … take consignments… I'd have to talk it over with Maggie. I'm sure we can agree on a small percentage."

Sounding more like herself then, Althea said, "All right, dear, whatever you decide will be fine with me."

"I have some free-time tomorrow morning. Do you want me to come over and mark the pieces you least mind parting with?"

"Yes, all right." Althea's gaze traveled over us, now resting side by side under the dining room table.

"Will you bring Murfy?"

"Sure, they seem to get along fine."

Simon and I looked at each other, pleased with their decision, looking forward to some playtime.

"And there'd no charge for the decorating advice," Alyx added.

"Oh, no; I can't let you do that. I don't want you to think I'm taking advantage of our friendship."

"I don't think that, Althea. Besides, the room has good bones," and to assess it better, she stood and looked around. "All it needs is some re-arranging. The only other suggestion I have is to remove the heavy drapery and leave the plantation shutters in place."

That appeared to be acceptable to Althea, so they agreed on a time for Alyx to come over the next day.

I was pensive on the ride back to the store. Simon was about my age, and ever so worldly. His previous human had been a diplomat and Simon had accompanied him all over the world, whereas, born only two blocks from my current residence, I'd lived in Beachside my whole life.

Simon said there was more to our kind than I knew of or had ever imagined. He said that we were not the same, but we were the same kind because we were both cats. What did he mean? I looked forward to our next meeting to learn the secrets to which he'd alluded.

Alyx pulled up at the rear of the store, and I focused on my job. The probable diamond thief had looked unsure of himself, nervous and scared. I figured he'd hidden the diamond in one of those little drawers in the desk and planned to return during the store's business hours to retrieve it rather than after hours—he didn't strike me as the breaking and entering type. I was confident that my housemates and I could take care of him. The girls had had some experience with that sort of thing already.

After a busy hour of alertness in the store, I took time out for a nap and was running a stationary marathon when I jerked awake, perplexed by my dream, which usually involved chasing someone or something. Periodically, I dream about fighting that scruffy cat that hangs out in the yard.

Since time isn't something cats are necessarily aware of or care about, I didn't know how long I'd been sleeping. I did want to know if we were going home soon, so I set off to get a sense of what was going on. Bernice was on the sales floor, Alyx was in the workroom sitting behind the desk working on something, and Maggie was at the worktable comparing fabric samples. I effortlessly jumped up on the desk and rubbed my head under Alyx's chin.

"Where have you been?"

I answered with a meow, pleased when she looked at her watch.

"I guess you've had enough for the day, huh?"

I'd always taken our communication for granted; now I wondered. Was this what Simon meant when he asked how my human knew what I wanted? How was it possible that we could communicate?

Alyx put away the rest of the things she was working on. "Murfy, go get Misty and we'll go home."

I trotted off to find Misty and heard Maggie say, "He's something else, you know. I think he understood what you said."

"Sometimes it makes you wonder, doesn't it?"

"To some blind souls all cats are much alike. To a cat lover every cat from the beginning of time has been utterly and amazingly unique."
—Jenny de Vries

CHAPTER FOUR: *More Than Somewhat Involved*

Alyx had met David Hunter eight months earlier, and had not been aware of her attraction for him during an awful ordeal that had brought them together. Afterwards, he'd kept in touch by visiting Antiques & Designs once or twice a month, purchasing several items along the way, such as a painting for his home and a scale of justice sculpture for his office.

When he mentioned to Alyx that he collected first edition books, she offered to help him locate one he said he'd had no success finding. Although books weren't her specialty, Alyx knew a dealer in rare books. It took months to find it and when she presented the book to David a week later, he invited her to dinner to celebrate.

Alyx denied being nervous about seeing Hunter—but I knew she was—she only made chamomile tea when she was nervous. While the tea steeped, she took off her beige linen skirt and striped green blouse that she was wearing, and slipped on her yellow terry bathrobe that was hanging from a hook behind the bathroom door. She carried her tea and the mail to the screened porch, also called the lanai. She passed through the living room, her favorite room in the house after she'd repainted the walls antique white and added colorful Oriental rugs over the original wood floor. The new patio door was flanked by two tall windows that provided much-needed light and a great view of the tropical landscaped backyard.

Her mail was the usual assortment of bills, credit card offers, advertisements, and more credit card offers. The only item of seeming interest was a short letter and a photo of a little girl, probably from her sister in Lansing, Michigan, where Alyx grew up and most of her family still lived.

She finished her tea, set the mail aside, and said to no one in particular, "I wonder when I'll get to be a grandmother."

Misty and Pooky followed her to the bedroom to watch her get ready, and informed me that she looked perfect, wearing an antique white silk blouse, brown slacks, and brown platform sandals.

The doorbell chimed Hunter's arrival. She opened the door, and he presented her with a pink rose in full bloom. "For a beautiful lady," he said.

She breathed in its fragrant scent and her cheeks turned the color of the rose. Hunter smiled sheepishly and stepped inside at her invitation. "It's from my garden, personally cultivated."

"I would never have guessed that you like to play in the dirt. Do you do general gardening or do you specialize in growing roses?"

"I do a little gardening for relaxation regrettably, not as much as I'd like."

"Let me put this in water, and I'm ready to go. Would you like to sit for a minute?"

"I'll wait here. Your cats will keep me company," he said, bending over to scratch my ear.

Alyx appeared calm. Any apprehension she might have felt on her first official date with Hunter appeared to be gone, and as much as I wanted to accompany her on her date, there was no way she was going to take me with her. I trusted Hunter to keep her safe, and I was sure I'd eventually hear all about it anyway.

As everybody knows, cats don't talk. However, we have other ways of communicating and often do, although never in the presence of humans. So following Alyx's departure, I had something to discuss with my housemates and we all gathered in the living room.

Even though Pooky wasn't interested in coming to the store with Misty and me every day, she still liked the treats that Alyx brought home from the store, and she loved hearing the stories Misty and I had to tell about our day at work. Misty bounced ahead, jumped on the couch, via the coffee table, and unable to wait any longer, relayed what had happened, embellishing the part about being stepped on, taking her time describing in detail what the man did to her. Pooky rolled her eyes and suggested that it would be better if I told the story, unless we wanted to be there all night.

Pooky, a long hair black cat with different colored eyes (one blue and one green) had put on a lot of weight since Alyx took her in as a stray. Totally out of character to Pooky's snide remark, Misty responded with an unkind comment about Pooky's weight problem.

Tired of the antagonism, I flicked my tail impatiently and demanded quiet. I didn't get their full attention until they heard me say that Alyx might be in danger. Pooky questioned what the robbery had to do with Alyx. I explained that I expected the thief to return to the store to get his diamond out of the desk. Pooky still didn't see how he was a threat to Alyx. I reminded them once again that the man was going to be angry with someone when he came back and didn't find the desk in the store. As an aside, Misty added that the man was a brute.

I said that we all needed to go with Alyx in the morning, to be on the lookout for the thief and be ready to protect her, Maggie or anyone else he might threaten. I don't know if Pooky understood or not, but all the same, she did agree to go. That settled, I waited for Hunter to bring Alyx back from the upscale Italian restaurant where he said he was taking her for dinner, one of two in the area with valet service.

Around nine o'clock, I heard Hunter's car engine and trotted to the front door. Hunter had his arm loosely around Alyx's waist as they walked up to the door laughing. Alyx said it was still early and asked him if he would like a cup of espresso coffee.

I knew that Alyx was very busy as a part owner of the antique store and design business, and she didn't have much of a social life, especially since Maggie had started seeing her friend, George. At the same time, Alyx's son Ethan had met someone who kept him occupied. Although Alyx never said, I knew there were times she was lonely. The felines and I did our best to keep her happy. Hunter seemed to be doing a better job of it, however, than we did, and I was pleased to see my human smiling and flirting.

"Do you have an espresso maker?" Hunter wanted to know.

"No, I have the old-fashioned espresso coffee pot that the general Italian population uses. I found it at a garage sale several years ago, and have used it ever since. The woman who sold it to me had no idea what it was. Funny how the whole world knows all about us and how we live, yet we are so ignorant of other countries and their cultures. You wouldn't expect that since we have so many different cultures within this country."

"To be honest, I never thought about it; you make a good point."

She gestured toward the couch, which was at that moment, free of cats. "Have a seat. I'll only be a minute."

He nodded and remained standing. "I love espresso coffee and since I'm one of those people ignorant of other cultures, can I see the kind of coffeepot you use?"

"Sure, I happen to have a collection of them."

"Why am I not surprised?" he said, following her. "Have you traveled to Italy?"

"No, I haven't, maybe one day I will. I had a friend in high school who was Italian, and she and her parents used to visit every year or two. Nina always came back with lots of pictures to share. I guess her love of her ancestral town built on the side of a mountain rubbed off on me."

"So, that's why you know all about espresso coffee pots," he said with a grin.

"Yes, I confess," she said, taking down two demitasse cups from a cabinet and setting them on a tray. She added two small spoons along with a bowl of sugar. She poured the dark, aromatic liquid, and Hunter carried the tray to the living room.

The conversation flowed smoothly. They talked of their work and their passions. He made her laugh when he told her about the first case he'd argued. After a while, Hunter put his coffee down and took her hand. "I've really enjoyed our time together tonight. I'm sorry it didn't happen sooner," he cleared his throat, "I... was somewhat involved with someone when I met you, and it's taken this long to settle it."

Her first reaction was confusion followed by disappointment. "I don't understand. When I invited you to my house before, for the celebration dinner, you said there was no wife or girlfriend. You've never mentioned anyone during any of the times we've spoken."

He nodded and tried to explain. "I was separated at the time…had been for six months. Joann had a hard time with it even though it was her idea. She kept me on a string for a long-time… until I forced the decision. The divorce was final two weeks ago."

"David, I'd say you were more than *somewhat involved.* I understand why you didn't tell me before— we never really discussed anything personal those few times you came in or we had coffee; I just assumed you were free," she said, pulling her hand away and reaching for the coffee.

"Do you have any children?"

"No, Joann didn't want any children."

"How long were you married?"

"Twenty years."

"Were you happy most of that time?"

"Yes and no. For a long time I loved her more than she loved me."

"How about you, were you happy most of the time you were married?"

"Yes, I was until the day Bob told me he didn't love me anymore."

She didn't have to tell him a whole lot more as he had learned everything about her while working on her son Ethan's case earlier that year.

"The evening has gone by too quickly," he said as she walked him to the door, and Alyx agreed.

"Thank you for a lovely evening, Alyx." He turned and kissed her lightly, his lips barely touching hers, the same way cats touch noses without actually making contact in greeting one another. I didn't need to see any more of that and trotted away.

I heard Alyx say, "Good night, David. I think you had better go. I'm not ready for anything more."

I didn't understand what that meant, but I didn't miss the disappointment in his sigh when he said, "Okay, Alyx... I'll be in touch."

The door closed and I sauntered back to the foyer. Alyx had her back pressed against the door. The look on her face when she went down on one knee to stroke my head wasn't one I expected. I liked Hunter, and I thought she liked him too—but now, even I—a stranger to romance—knew something was amiss.

*"Some cats is blind. And stone-deaf some. But ain't no
cat wuz ever dumb."*
—Anthony Ewer

CHAPTER FIVE: *Something Wrong*

The day began as it usually did; our routine the same as the day before, except that when Alyx was ready to leave, all three of us followed her to the truck.

"Okay, I get it. You all want to go today, right?"

The cottage-style bungalow where we live is located in the historic district of Beachside, about two blocks from the store. The neighborhood, still in the process of redevelopment, is a mix of architectural styles as the people living there are a mix of ages, young couples with children, middle-aged and retired folks who have lived there many years, and a handful of Florida natives.

Pooky took the ride better than I expected—she was only slightly hyperventilating when we arrived at the store a few minutes later. Bernice, a thirty-something, flamboyant dresser, and middle-aged Nelda, her opposite and equally competent employee, were already there. Bernice helped with the carriers; no small feat since I alone weigh sixteen pounds more or less, and I think it's probably more rather than less.

Nelda made the mistake of reaching for Pooky and got her hand smacked as a gentle warning not to touch.

"Don't mind her, Nelda, she's like that with everybody; she's not as sociable as the other two cats," said Alyx. "You'd think she'd want to stay home—she was the first one out."

"Thanks for the warning. I'll make sure the customers leave her alone too."

It had been a while since Pooky was in the store last, and she took off sniffing and touching, investigating her surroundings.

"You know that you and Bernice will be here by yourselves for most of the day, right? I promised Althea I'd help her redecorate her living room, and I expect to be there all morning and maybe through lunch."

"That won't be a problem. Bernice and I can handle the customers, and we'll watch the cats."

"I'm taking Murfy with me, so he can play with her cat Simon while I work. Althea thinks her cat needs a playmate."

Nelda laughed. "The notion that a cat needs anybody, even another cat, is hilarious."

More than a half-hour later, Alyx was still trying to reach Althea on the phone to confirm our visit.

Bernice caught up with her when her customer walked away and asked if she was still going to Althea's place.

"I've been calling for the past thirty minutes and she's not answering her phone. I'm a little worried about her."

"Maybe she ran out to get something," offered Bernice by way of explanation.

"She's expecting me; I don't think she'd leave without calling. I hope you're right."

Alyx kept trying to reach Althea without success, giving Misty and Pooky the opportunity to corner me and let me know that they didn't appreciate the fact that I'd dragged them to the store claiming it was important, and then I take off on a play date.

They were right to be angry. I should have explained. I apologized for my error, and I know from their silence that my apology wasn't accepted. No matter, we still had a job to do, and I told them what to look for and what to do if the thief came back.

"As every cat owner knows, no one owns a cat."
—Ellen Perry Berkeley

CHAPTER SIX: *No Need to Hurry*

Althea lived in a condominium community on the river, minutes from the new bridge. Althea's car was in the driveway, so Alyx parked in the space reserved for visitors. She rang the bell several times, knocked, and there was still no answer. She tried the door and amazingly it opened.

"Hello? Althea, it's me, Alyx, are you home?" The stillness was unsettling. Aware that a cat lived there, Alyx closed the door behind us. She called again. No answer. She moved slowly into the living room and there was Althea, crumpled in a heap at the foot of the stairs. Alyx unceremoniously deposited the carrier with me in it where she stood, and crossed the short distance in a heartbeat. But I knew there was no need to hurry. Althea was dead.

A short time later, the police arrived. I immediately recognized Detective Smarts. He had wrongfully arrested Alyx's son Ethan earlier in the year, and I hadn't forgotten. I didn't think much of his detective skills and I openly expressed my feelings. That is to say, I hissed and snarled at him. He practically snarled back. Alyx, on the other hand, politely answered his questions, telling him what she knew, keeping her feelings to herself.

Smarts asked her if Althea had any relatives.

"She did mention one niece, her husband's niece, actually."

"Do you know her name or where she lives?"

"Her first name is Carole. Her last name sounds like *dirt*—no wait—*earth*. That's it! Carole Berth and I think she lives in Umatilla."

He wrote it all down and flipped the page. "Why are you here, Ms. Hille?"

Alyx hesitated before answering. "Althea asked me to help her get rid of some of her furniture and redecorate her condominium. We had made an appointment for today. I called several times to confirm my visit, and when I didn't reach her, I got worried and came over anyway. The rest I've already told you."

"One question, Ms. Hille. I have an appreciation for antiques, and know the value of some of these pieces. Just how were you going to help her get *rid* of some of the furniture?"

"What I meant was that I would buy some pieces and take the rest on consignment," she answered pleasantly.

He closed his notebook, and Alyx asked, "Are we finished here? Am I free to go?"

"We have to get your fingerprints, and then you can go."

"Why do you need my prints?" she asked suspiciously.

"It's procedure, Ms. Hille."

"What about her cat? A Siamese. I'd like to look for him and take him home with me. That's okay, isn't it?"

"Other than filing some paperwork with the Humane Society, I don't see why not. Go ahead and look for the cat, and I'll go find someone to take your prints."

She stood, and sat back down again. The detective saw the pallor in her cheeks and offered to get her a glass of ice water, which she accepted.

"Would you like me to call someone for you?"

"No, thank you. I need to sit for a few minutes, and I'll be fine. Thanks for the water."

Simon was nowhere to be found, and so we left immediately after a uniformed officer took Alyx's fingerprints. Smarts was in the room the whole time, and I didn't like the way he was looking at me. For a second, he had me thinking that he was going to have me paw-printed as well.

As soon as we drove away, Alyx called Maggie. She had been all right up until that point, and then when she told Maggie that Althea was dead, her eyes filled with tears, and she pulled off to the side of the road for a few minutes.

"I was going to bring her cat home with me, and I couldn't find him."

"He'll probably reappear when he's hungry."

"Yes, except I won't be there to see him."

"I'll swing over there on my way in tomorrow morning, and for the rest of the week, all right?"

"Thank you, Maggie."

We stopped at her store only long enough to pick up Misty and Pooky. Once home, the felines and I trooped out to the lanai, where the girls barraged me with questions. Did Althea's cat know what had happened? Was he upset? Who was taking care of him? I told them we hadn't found Simon. Then I asked Misty what had happened in the shop while we were gone. She communicated that she was on the counter by the front door the whole time that I was gone, and didn't see the thief or any other suspicious-looking person. The most exciting thing that happened was that Pooky got stuck in an open drawer she was inspecting. Pooky didn't think it was very amusing and swatted Misty.

The communication came to a halt when Alyx came out on the lanai with a tuna salad sandwich. She ate half her sandwich and put the rest on her plate. I jumped on her lap and licked her hand, offering comfort as best I could, hoping for a taste of tuna. The others hunched quietly nearby for the same reason, also hoping for some leftovers. Then the home phone rang, and I positioned myself to hear the conversation—something I regularly do so I know what's going on.

"Are you all right, Alyx?" Hunter asked when Alyx answered, pressing the button for speakerphone.

"How did you know I was home?"

"When you didn't answer your cell phone I called the store. Bernice told me about Althea and that you'd gone home. I'm sorry. I know you were fond of her," he said, "It must have been awful for you, finding her body."

His voice was kind. Alyx sank deeper into my favorite chair and laid her head back. They talked a while and made a tentative date for later in the week. Alyx looked around the room she loved. She told Maggie that the mix of old, new and antiques together with the wood floor covered in colorful antique rugs made her feel grounded. She had brought work home with her and stayed busy the rest of the afternoon, detailing her part of the renovation for the arrogant new client who wanted her million-dollar home restored to its 1930s splendor.

The beachside home had deteriorated through neglect, and Alyx was thrilled when the home went up for sale. She had told Ethan that she hoped the new owners would restore it rather than have it razed. Maggie was clearly not impressed with the new owner, Linda Stone and told her so. Nevertheless, Alyx wanted to work on the house and Maggie agreed to take on the job, accepting her argument that the profit would be worth the effort—an odd argument coming from Alyx or Maggie for that matter.

"Most beds sleep up to six cats. Ten cats without the owner."
—Stephen Baker

CHAPTER SEVEN: *A Pioneer Christmas*

Alyx found the perfect lamp she'd been looking for on-line, completed the transaction and logged off when a car came up the drive. Before she could get to the door, she heard Ethan's familiar greeting, "Hi, Mom; it's me—your one and only son."

"Hi, honey. I'm in the office."

Misty pawed Ethan's pockets for the expected treat he always brought whenever he visited, and we weren't disappointed with the tasty morsels he produced. About six feet tall, with blue eyes, short black hair and a thin-line beard, Ethan, considered handsome by human female standards, gave his mother a hug and a quick kiss on the cheek.

"I've missed you... been busy?" she asked casually.

"Sorry I haven't been over, Mom. Nikki and I went to South Beach for a couple of days."

"You could have told me that when I called you instead of letting me wonder what was going on."

"Yeah, I know. You always worry when I tell you I'm going out of town, and I didn't want you to worry. Besides, I'm twenty-three," he said, putting his arm around her shoulders, "I shouldn't have to tell my mother everything I do."

Having had only each other since her divorce years earlier, the mother-child bond was strong—except Ethan was no longer a child. Occasionally, Alyx had trouble remembering that, this time she did remember and wisely said no more on the subject other than, "I'm glad you're back safe and sound."

She served the cherry pie she'd picked up from the bakery, at the kitchen table where a bank of windows framed a perfect Southern picture—a huge magnolia tree with a white wrought iron bench sitting under its shady canopy. Alyx had designed the kitchen around the enamel-topped, 1940's table and chairs that had been in her parent's basement and that still held pleasant memories of the many family gatherings that had taken place while her parents were still living.

She told Ethan about Althea. "It was only yesterday that she was making plans for her future, for starting a new life."

He asked if she knew the actual cause of death.

"No, I don't. The fact is, I may never know."

She mentioned Simon, the missing cat. "I know Althea would want me to make sure he has a home. But I don't want another cat." She gave him one of her special smiles, "How would you like to have a sleek, handsome Siamese cat?"

I liked the idea and tapped my tail. Misty saw my reaction and turned her back to me in obvious disapproval.

"Maybe, if he's anything like Murfy."

"I'll let you know if he turns up."

"Mom, I'm not promising. ..."

"I know," she said as she cleared the table. "So do you have plans for this week-end?"

"Yes. Nikki read in the paper that the old pioneer settlement is hosting its annual *A Florida Christmas.*

Neither one of us has been there since we were in high school."

"What did the article say about the event?"

"She said the historic buildings in the settlement are decked with old-fashioned pioneer ornaments. There's music, including concerts in the 1890 church and visitors can join carolers as they stroll around the grounds."

"That place is like a tiny rural village, isn't it? I think the oldest building is the 1875 log cabin. My favorite is the kitchen in the old schoolhouse. I love the high ceiling with tall windows all along the wall looking out to the herb garden, not to mention the fresh-baked goods they offer."

"My favorite was the blacksmith shop. I think I was intrigued by the red hot iron being pounded into something."

"Well, it sounds like fun. All you need is some cool weather to make it perfect."

"Yeah, that's what Nikki said. Did they have sour orangeade the last time you went?"

"No, and it doesn't sound like something I would want either," she said, puckering her lips. "What is it?"

Ethan laughed. "Nikki said it's an old Florida pioneer treat made from the juice of sour oranges."

"Well, that's a new one on me. I've never heard of sour orange trees, unless they mean from un-ripened oranges. Let me know what it tastes like."

"I'll do better than that. I'll bring you some.

"A cat's eyes are windows enabling us to see into
another world."
—Irish Legend

CHAPTER EIGHT: *The Crime Is Murder*

Sunday was Alyx's turn to be on the sales floor and Maggie's day off. They rotated their schedules so that everyone had two consecutive days off, if not necessarily the same two days, every week. However, it didn't always work out that way for Alyx and Maggie. Sometimes, one or the other worked seven days in a row taking time off only when necessary. They would be first to tell you that the hard work and sacrifice paid off. They had achieved their dream, and Alyx had said more than once that they were more successful than either of them had ever expected. In fact, there had been some discussion about opening another store. As far as I knew, the discussion had ended there.

The customer at the cash register now, obviously excited about his purchase, was telling Alyx how thrilled his wife was going to be when he gave her the California Pottery oblong platter in her pattern—roses and tulips in mauve. Alyx wrapped the plate and bagged it in the new, expensive, brown paper gift bags with the name of the store and picture of the store's façade printed on one side of the bag.

Detective Smarts and another man walked in just as she completed the sales transaction, and she directed the two men to the workroom at the rear of the store, recently rearranged to make room for a couch and worktable. I followed discreetly.

Alyx sat at her desk. Detective Smarts, wearing dress slacks, a button-down, long-sleeved shirt and no tie, introduced his partner whose name I missed. I didn't miss his sharp creased slacks and crisp blue shirt. The officers pulled up two chairs and sat facing Alyx. I perched on the worktable behind them, keeping a cautious eye on the two men.

"I'll come straight to the point, Ms. Hille. We're investigating a homicide. Mrs. Burns was murdered."

"What? How?"

"She was smothered."

"Smothered? How do you know that?" Alyx asked incredulously.

The detective rubbed his forehead. "Ms. Hille, I'm not going to get technical here. Among other signs, the medical examiner found bruising around her mouth, and her eyes were bloodshot."

Alyx shook her head. "Who would want to kill a sweet lady like Althea?"

"That's what we aim to find out, ma'am," said the sharp dresser as he unclipped a ballpoint pen from his clipboard, poised to take down her every word.

"I'll be glad to help you in any way I can, but I've already told you all I know."

Detective Smarts inhaled deeply. He rubbed his forehead again. "Yes, and by telling me again, you might remember something you didn't remember before."

"Okay, I understand. What do you want to know?"

Smarts asked all the questions; his partner took notes.

"How well did you know her?"

"I met her last spring when she came in the store. The slant-front desk in the window display drew her in;

after that, she came in every month to make a payment, and often to browse or chat. Maggie and I had lunch with her about once a month, usually at the café next door."

"Were you ever at her residence?"

"Friday, when George and I delivered her desk was the first time."

"George, who?"

"George Lucas is the woodworker we use to restore antiques or create new items from things that had a previous life as something else. Do you need his address or phone number?"

"No, we can get that."

"You said she saw the desk last spring. Why did it take so long for her to get it?"

"She said she didn't have the money to pay for it and didn't want to put it on a credit card, so we arranged monthly payments. She was a proud lady and wouldn't take it home until it was paid for in full."

He looked at his partner and at his notepad to make sure he was keeping up with the notes and continued when he got a nod.

"According to our information, Mrs. Burns was a wealthy woman, meaning that she could have paid for the desk at anytime."

"That may be true, and I don't doubt it is. All I can tell you is what she told me."

Detective Smarts stood up and his partner followed suit, hooking his pen back on the clipboard rather than putting it his shirt pocket, as most men would do.

They thanked her for her time and left.

Misty had been listening at the door, and heaved a big sigh of relief after I let her know that Smarts was investigating Althea's murder and wasn't after our humans.

*"Cats are rather delicate creatures and they are subject
to a lot of ailments, but I never heard of one who
suffered from insomnia."*
—Joseph Wood Crutch

CHAPTER NINE: *Althea's Secret Life*

Since Misty was the only one of us cats who'd seen
the thief with and without his disguise, it made sense to
post her at the front door, with Pooky nearby for
reinforcement. The only napping allowed were catnaps,
and that didn't make anybody happy.

The well-dressed woman now standing at the
counter ruined my first catnap of the day. I sensed an
aura of suspense surrounding her and looked her over
carefully.

Alyx asked her if she needed assistance.

"Yes, I'm looking for Alyx Hille."

"I'm Alyx. How can I help you?"

I assumed the woman was there to see her about a
decorating job—she wasn't. She introduced herself as
Carole Berth, Althea's niece.

"It's nice to meet you, Carole," said Alyx. "I wish
we'd met under different circumstances. I'm sorry
about your aunt; she was a lovely lady and will be
missed."

"I didn't see or speak to my aunt often, so I don't
know if she has any friends. She mentioned your name
the last time I spoke to her. I know you've been kind to
her, and I wanted to thank you and let you know that

there are no funeral arrangements; Detective Smarts said you asked."

Alyx nodded her head, and Carole continued. She's simply going to be buried at Shady Rest's convenience."

"I did ask Detective Smarts," replied Alyx, "and thank you for letting me know."

"Did my aunt tell you much about herself?"

"No, not very much. I met her last spring when she saw the desk in the window. She came in to look and we chatted for a while. She seemed lonely, and I invited her to come back any time. Sometimes she came in to browse, and other times to talk. Maggie, my business partner, and I tried to have lunch with her about once a month."

"Did she tell you she was in a mental institution for ten years because of that desk, or I should say, one like it?"

"No, she didn't," answered Alyx.

I wondered why this woman was revealing Althea's intimate secrets to Alyx, and at the same time, intrigued by what she was saying.

After several customers came in the store, looked in their direction, and impatiently waited for assistance, Alyx suggested to Carole that they move to the workroom for privacy.

Carole took a seat on the couch and Alyx joined her, with me tailing behind. "Why did she move from Umatilla? Althea never said."

"When my uncle died," explained Carole, "Aunt Althea packed up and moved away. I was okay with it until she told me about the desk in your store."

"I don't understand. What bothered you about the desk?"

Carole took a deep breath, looked around the room, spotted the coffee pot, and asked if she could have a cup. Alyx apologized for not asking her sooner, and quickly stepped to the credenza, filled a mug with black coffee as requested, brought the mug back to her seat, and handed it to Carole.

"Did she tell you about the one like it that she'd purchased in Africa?"

"She told me that her husband—your uncle—was an overseer in a counting house for a diamond mining company. She said she joined him in Sierra Leone shortly after they were married, and while on their honeymoon, they attended an auction where she saw a desk like the one here in our store, and fell in love with it."

"Did she tell you about the diamond hidden in the desk?"

"Yes. Althea shared the story with me and Maggie more than once, and it never varied, which led me to believe that maybe some of it was true."

I too had heard the story once or twice about a young man who worked in the diamond mines and who fell in love with the daughter of a rich diamond company executive. Her father forbade the relationship, and they decided to run away. The young man stole a diamond, the means to their happiness together, and brought it to her. She had the diamond in her hand when the company guards burst in and shot him. They said that she hid the diamond in the desk as a reminder of his love, and so no one could ever prove that he stole it. She didn't want her unborn child's father branded as a thief. She never married and kept the desk until she died.

"More than likely," explained Carole, "the story was fabricated by the auctioneer in order to get more bidders. My uncle said that from the time Aunt Althea brought that desk home, she became obsessed with finding the hidden diamond. She was positive there was a secret compartment where the diamond was hidden."

"I never would have thought wealth meant that much to her," said Alyx.

"It didn't. Finding the diamond did."

"She told me the desk burned down with the house after they left Sierra Leone. Is that true?" asked Alyx.

"Yes," replied Carole, "it's true the desk burned, but it was my uncle who burned it. That's when she really lost it and my uncle had to put her in a private institution."

"Did your uncle blame her for what happened?"

"No, not her—the desk. You see, about a year after she acquired the desk, their two-month-old son disappeared from his room. Althea was home and said she didn't hear anything; she was in the living room searching for the hidden diamond in the desk."

Alyx's hand flew to cover her gaping mouth.

"She never told you about it, did she?"

Alyx shook her head. "What happened to the baby?"

"My uncle paid the kidnappers the ransom they demanded—but they never saw their child again—dead or alive."

Carole took several sips of coffee and Alyx waited for her to continue.

"When she saw the desk in your shop window, she called me. She was so excited, she could hardly speak."

"Now, wait a minute," Alyx interrupted, "She told me her original desk burned. She didn't really think our desk was the same desk, did she?"

Carole shrugged and reached for the mug, and held it aloft for a few seconds before she took a sip and set it down again.

"I don't know. She never said she did; but in her crazy, confused state of mind, who knows." Carole stood and placed the coffee mug on the credenza. "Her will stipulates that everything is to go to me upon her death. I don't want or need any of her things, and that's why I'm here. Would you be interested in buying the contents of the condominium?"

"Well, maybe not everything. Some of the pieces for sure—if we can agree on a price."

Carole opened her elegant Gucci purse and took out a key. "I would like for you to determine what it's all worth and send me a check. In fact, keep the key until everything is gone and mail it back with the check. If you don't mind, I'd appreciate it if you'd organize and box her papers and such, and leave those for me. Then all I have to worry about is selling her condominium. Detective Smarts said you were also interested in taking her cat. I didn't know she had one."

"She told me he appeared at her door at about the same time she first came into our shop."

"Well, if you find him, he's yours," concluded Carole.

Two thoughts came to my mind upon hearing this conversation: Was Althea's death somehow connected to the diamond stolen from Hall's Jewelry? Or was it something else altogether? After hearing what Althea's niece had to say, I now had my doubts. What if in her twisted thinking, Althea believed that the desk in our shop was the same desk that she'd had in Africa, and she'd told someone here in Beachside about the diamond in the desk story?

*"If you want to know the character of a man, find out
what his cat thinks of him."*
—Anonymous

CHAPTER TEN: *Simon's Nocturnal Visit*

David Hunter rang the doorbell and stepped back.
Alyx hurried to the foyer, peered in the mirror, fluffed
her hair, and added color to her lips before she opened
the door.

"Hi, David, come in. I wasn't expecting you for
another twenty minutes."

"I can leave and come back later, if you'd like."

"No—it's fine. I'm ready to go, if you are."

"Good. The restaurant is well known for fresh
seafood and is usually crowded. I'm sure tonight will be
no exception. They don't take reservations, so I came a
little early if you'd like to have a drink on the deck
while we wait for a table."

"Sitting outside on the deck with a glass of wine
sounds wonderful, even if it's too dark for an ocean
view."

"I'm glad to see you look much better than you
sounded when I spoke to you the other day."

"It was a shock finding Althea like that. She was
murdered you know."

"No, I didn't know. How did you find that out?"

"Detective Smarts came to ask me more questions,
and he told me."

The lawyer in David prompted him to ask several questions of his own, I surmised from my perch on top of the sofa.

"I'll be glad to go to the funeral with you, if you like."

"There won't be one. Her niece came to see me today and said Shady Rest will simply bury her at their convenience when her body is released."

"That's not very common, is it?"

Alyx shrugged, "No, not really. Carole—that's her niece—told me some interesting things about Althea. I'll tell you on the way. I'm ready for that glass of wine."

On their way out, Hunter looked at me and asked what the girls and I had been up to, and Alyx told him about all of us cats accompanying her to the store every day.

"Maybe they know something about this case that no one else knows," he said with what I thought was a serious face. Was that an invitation for us to get involved?

Alyx hesitated before she responded, "You may be right. Nothing Murfy does is a surprise to me anymore."

Was she thinking the same thing?

Keeping track of all the goings-on at the store, plus dodging the reaching hands of those who wanted to hold, and in a few cases, pull our tails, made the day an exhausting one. It had been especially trying one for Pooky, who was still sprawled on her back in the middle of the living room where she'd tossed herself on our arrival home.

As tired as I was, I waited for Alyx to come home. And as tired as I was, I thought I'd sleep all night; but I didn't. In the quiet hours of the morning, after the night owls had gone to bed, and the day workers hadn't yet arrived, I decided to sit out on the screened porch for a while. Alyx kept the pet door locked at night and when she wasn't home during the day—I knew how to unlock the pet door and was out on the lanai within seconds.

I heard a sound, and my ears swiveled to identify the location of the sound. I stood on my hind legs at the screen door for a better view, and the fur on my back stood up when I saw a rustling of the tall ferns surrounding the small brick patio outside the door. A low growl, deep in my throat warned the intruder. Suddenly, the ferns parted, and Simon landed directly in front of me. I had no idea how he knew where we lived and when I asked, he smiled a secret smile and let me know that I had a lot to learn about our kind. He beckoned me to follow him where we could talk. He understood my reluctance to disobey my human, and at the same time, I saw the wisdom in distancing ourselves from the house next door when Smoochie, the Pomeranian, decided to reveal his presence with several loud successive barks.

The locked screen door that posed a problem for me was not a problem for Simon. He slyly unsheathed his front claws ready to slit the screen. Naturally, I was shocked at his destructive suggestion. Simon arched his back and rubbed his side against the doorjamb. He reiterated what he'd said before about learning what our kind could do for our humans. He convinced me it was necessary, and I suggested he do it in the corner, behind the larger potted plants, where it was a less noticeable. I winced as he sliced a clean straight line down the screen, all the while unable to resist watching his efforts.

Soon, I heard scampering behind me, and looked over my shoulder to see Misty and Pooky lurking in the shadows of the potted plants in the lanai. The half-moon in the clear sky lit up the yard giving the two ladies a clear view of Simon and me.

Among the three of us at home, Misty slept the least amount of time. Keeping everyone—humans and cats––company, kept her too busy to nap during the day. She usually made up for lost sleep at night. That night, she was still awake in the lanai when I returned. I deliberately ignored her as I sauntered past, and she meekly followed me inside.

Simon had given me a lot to think about—and a big decision to make.

The next morning, Alyx tried to roll out of bed, and couldn't move. Pooky and Misty had her trapped under the covers. She reached out to the closest cat, which happened to be Pooky stretched along her hip, and tried to push her aside. Pooky didn't budge.

Alyx squinted at the bedside clock, yawned, and went back to sleep until we decided it really was time for her to get up. I followed her to the kitchen where the other two felines waited for their breakfast. She refilled their food and water bowls, made coffee, and sat at the kitchen table watching us while she waited for the coffee drip cycle to finish.

"Pooky, there's no question about it; you're getting too fat, and we have to fix that; it's not healthy for you, kitty-cat."

The gurgle of the coffee maker told her the coffee was ready. She filled her travel mug, took it to the living room, and watched the local news.

Breakfast nibbling over, the felines ran to the living room, playing hopscotch on the way, and draped themselves on the back of the couch and chair. An hour later, Alyx was ready for work and so were we. She refilled her travel mug, and we filed out to the truck, all set for another day at the store.

Alyx, who was the first to arrive and busy setting up, didn't hear Nelda noiselessly walk up behind her.

"Good morning," Nelda said rather loudly.

Alyx jumped, and my housemates scattered. "Nelda, you startled me. I didn't hear you come in."

"Sorry; next time I'll be sure to slam the door," she kidded. "I see all your kitty-cats are with you, or I should say they were until I scared them away."

"I don't know what got into them; they all insisted on coming—and here they are," she said, stepping aside as Nelda rearranged a couple of chairs that were deliberately blocking the entrance.

"Well, judging from the treats the customers bring them, they sure like having them around. These cats have enough to keep them fat and happy for a year."

Alyx reached for a plastic bag under the counter. "Thanks for reminding me. My cats don't need all this food, especially Pooky, and I can't give the other two a treat and not her. What I'm going to do is bag what's here and bring it to the animal shelter around the block."

It was a noble gesture on her part, yet so disappointing for us to see the basket empty.

"Any cat that misses a mouse pretends it was aiming for the dead leaf."
—Charlotte Gray

CHAPTER ELEVEN: *Family Portraits Arouse Suspicion*

Alyx and Maggie were having breakfast, and Maggie asked when they were going to start evaluating Althea's things.

"I was thinking of going over there tomorrow for a preliminary inventory. Her niece made it very clear she wants this wrapped up as soon as possible," said Alyx.

They discussed what they were going to do and decided to buy the antique pieces and conduct an estates sale for the rest of the items on the premises. Alyx said she would mark the pieces accordingly.

"Do you want me to come with you?"

"No, I think I can handle it alone."

"Are you sure you don't mind being there by yourself?"

"I'll be fine. Besides, you have plans for the day. You don't need to be spending your time babysitting me."

"Okay, if you're sure. Too bad her cat never turned up."

"Yes, it is. I hope someone found him and gave him a home. He's a handsome cat, and I know you don't usually hear this about cats, but I thought he had an intelligent look in his eyes."

"I think a cat is a cat except for Murfy—he's something else—my imagination doesn't take me farther than that."

That observation of my special skills was fine with me—the less people suspected, the better I could do my job.

First thing the following morning, Alyx drove to Althea's condominium with me riding along in my carrier. Althea's car was gone, so Alyx parked in the driveway. I assumed someone had moved Althea's car into the garage—more than likely, her niece had sold it.

As Alyx headed for the front door with me in tow in my carrier, she greeted an elderly man sweeping his driveway.

"No one's home," he said as he leaned on his push broom and squinted at Alyx. "I don't think I've seen you before. Are you a relative?"

"No, I'm a friend. I'm the one who found her body."

"I heard she was murdered. Why would anyone want to kill her? I don't know. This is such a crazy world; can't trust anybody, no more. Most residents living here are over 65-years old, you know, and this has us all scared. I don't like it when you have to be suspicious of everybody." He shook his head, "No, sir, I don't like it one bit."

Alyx stepped over the strip of grass separating the two driveways and introduced herself to the stooped gentleman who had a full head of white hair and cloudy blue eyes—remnants of a once young, handsome face.

"My name's William, William Emmett. You can call me Bill."

"It's nice to meet you, Bill. How well did you know Althea?"

He shrugged his bony shoulders, "She wasn't very friendly, kept mostly to herself except for when that cat of hers ran out. That's when she'd talk to the neighbors—when she went looking for him."

"That's what I was going to ask you about. Apparently, the cat ran away again. He wasn't in the house when I found Althea. A friend of mine has been checking every day, with no sign of Simon. Have you seen him by any chance?"

"No, I didn't know he was missing. I thought someone had taken him in."

"Well, I know Althea would want someone to take care of her cat, so if you do see him hanging around, I'll appreciate it if you give me a call."

She pulled a business card from her purse and handed it to him.

"I'll be sure to do that." He squinted at the card and put it in his pants pocket. "Did her niece inherit everything?"

"That's what she said."

"So she's gonna sell this place?"

"Yes, I think so."

He rubbed the top of his head in a circular motion. "Now...doesn't it take some time for all that to go through the court and all before she can do anything?"

"All I know is that she's the executor of the estate, so I think she can do whatever she wants."

He nodded, not fully convinced. "Didn't mean to be nosy. I was just wondering that's all."

Bill was quite a talker, and I realized that if Alyx didn't make a move soon, she'd become his captive audience, so I let myself be heard.

"That's my cat Murfy letting me know he wants to be let out of his carrier. Nice talking to you Bill. My friend Maggie and I own Antiques & Designs on Ocean Street. Althea's niece has asked us to dispose of the contents of her condominium, so you'll be seeing me again."

She unlocked the front door of Althea's house, and froze to the spot for a moment. It was evident the police had not conducted a neat and orderly investigation. It was disappointing that they had not shown a little more respect for the dead woman. Then again, maybe this was as neat as they were when they searched for evidence.

Alyx let me out of the carrier before she took the self-adhesive tags out of her tote bag and started inspecting each piece of furniture, marking those that Antiques & Designs wanted to buy for re-sale in the store, the first piece being the slant-front desk. Did Althea really think it was the same desk that she'd purchased all those years ago in Sierra Leone? Apparently, her story about the desk burning when the house caught fire was a lie.

Eventually, Alyx finished tagging items on the first floor and we moved on to the second floor. I was right behind her. Alyx looked confused as she stood in front of the portraits still hanging in the guest room. She took them down and put the portraits in the truck when she finished tagging the estate sale items on the second floor. Then, she took a walk around the outside of the building; I presumed she was looking for Simon. When she came around to the front, she waved at Bill, and we left.

When we returned to the shop, it was late morning, and Maggie hadn't left for the day yet. Alyx asked if she had time to discuss a figure for Althea's furniture and pick a date for the estate sale. Maggie said she did and when they decided that they couldn't do it for another three weeks, Alyx told her about the family portraits that had been left hanging on the wall.

"Do you think you can get along without me tomorrow? I'd like to take the portraits to Althea's niece and I don't know how much time I'll need."

"Sure, that's fine, except … why are you going?"

"Okay, I think there's more to this than it appears. Don't you think it's odd for Carole to leave the family portraits for the estate sale?"

"Not really. Maybe she didn't know the people."

"Yes, she did, Althea told me who they all were. One is Althea and her husband on their wedding day and the other is Carole's grandparents."

"Alyx, not everyone has an appreciation of their ancestry, you know."

"I know, yet something doesn't seem right. I learned from her next-door neighbor that Althea had several visitors the day before I found her body."

"Really. Who were they?"

"Carole and her son, Carole's son and another man, and a different man whom he couldn't identify—he only saw him from the back as he was leaving."

"Do you even know where Umatilla is?"

"I know that it's west of here. I have a GPS, I'm sure I'll find it."

"Okay, Alyx," Maggie sighed, "No use trying to talk you out of it. Drive carefully; you know how bad the highway traffic can get."

"Yes, I know. Unfortunately, it's the only east-west highway. It seems that road has been under construction forever—long enough to build a new one, I'd say. Of course, by the time they finish the new road, traffic will have doubled again."

The rest of the day at the store was uneventful. On the way home that evening, Alyx stopped at the supermarket and came out with a bag of unknown cat food. She filled one of the bowls at home with the new food, and we ran to sniff and taste. Misty and I agreed it was pretty awful, turned tail, and left Pooky crunching away as if it was her last meal. Her behavior was understandable though—she'd experienced hunger and nearly starved to death when her humans abandoned her by the side of a busy road. Misty and I have never experienced hunger; our bowl is always full. We let Alyx know when it isn't.

*"Your cat may never have to hunt farther than the
kitchen counter for its supper nor face a predator
fiercer than the vacuum cleaner."*
—Barbara L. Diamond

CHAPTER TWELVE: *A Disappointing Trip*

Something jarred me awake. I opened my eyes and
saw Misty hunched down on all fours, her face only
inches from mine. Annoyed at being disturbed, I flicked
the tip of my tail. She insisted I sit up as she had
something to say and wanted to be sure that I heard it. I
indulged her request and started washing the sleep out
of my eyes. She asked a legitimate question; I gave her
a legitimate answer.

Relentless in her pursuit for answers, she demanded
to know why I didn't go with Alyx to Umatilla. I said I
didn't see any reason to go. She didn't understand why
I wasn't concerned about Alyx any longer since nothing
had changed. I had nothing to say and started to walk
away. She persisted. Who was the cat that I'd spent the
night with and why did I let him slit the screen? She
wasn't going to like the answer, so I said that I didn't
want to discuss that either.

Misty relied on me to explain things to her things
about human and cat behaviors, and she made it clear
that she didn't understand, and that there couldn't
possibly be an explanation for my behavior of late.

I knew she was confused, yet I couldn't tell her of
the conflict raging within me—there was so much that

Simon said he could teach me. He confirmed what I'd suspected all along, that all cats have a purpose, and that is to provide comfort to humans, even if it's just to purr. I learned that some cats possess better developed senses and can do more for their humans than others do—in some cases, actually protect them from harm. I wanted to know how.

You see, before I adopted Alyx, my mother told me that the *M* on my forehead made me special in the same way that it made my father special. She said he was a Felis catus genius and since I had the same mark, so was I. Sad to say, I never met my father. He was picked up as a stray by Animal Control before I was born—one of the dangers of being an outdoor cat even if you're a genius.

Maybe my mother was right about the genius part. I did have a better understanding of humans and the laws that governed them than my housemates did, and I could do things that never even occurred to them. I concluded that since there are levels of intelligence for humans, this could also be true for cats.

Misty moved away, pulled her string closer, and held it securely in both paws. Pooky, who'd been grooming her tail, pretending not to be listening, curled up by her side—close, though not so close that one might think it was intentional.

I knew Misty was hurt and disappointed, and I did think she deserved an explanation; nevertheless, there was so much going on right now that I was distracted from doing the right thing.

Alyx came home from Umatilla around noon. I heard her ask Misty why she looked so sad, and I sauntered out to the living room. I stayed out of the way while she played with Misty and her string—an athletic shoelace Ethan had given her when he couldn't keep her away from his shoes. Misty was obsessed with it. If she wasn't dragging it, she was laying on it, and don't anyone dare touch it without her permission.

A few minutes later, Misty walked away bored, dragging her string behind her. Alyx headed to her bedroom and came out in her grungy housecleaning clothes. She headed for the kitchen, and we heard a big sigh, big enough to get our attention—all of us wondering whose mess she was cleaning up. Of course, no one wanted to look like the guilty party, so no one went to check it out.

I expected to see Alyx come out of the kitchen with her bucket of cleaning supplies. Instead, she grabbed the cordless phone and took it to the living room. I positioned myself on the back of the couch near her head so I could hear the speaker on the other end.

"Hi, Maggie, has it been very busy?"

"Why? You want to come in?"

"Not necessarily, but you know I'll be there if you say so."

"I'm kidding. The three of us can handle it. Next week, we reevaluate, right?"

"Right."

"How was your trip to Umatilla?"

"The ride was uneventful. No aggressive drivers flashing their lights at me to get out of the way because I was driving the speed limit instead of the twenty miles over they were doing. For a change, there were no accidents to slow down traffic or bring it to a complete standstill. It actually turned out to be a pleasant drive."

"Did you have any trouble finding the house?"

"It's not hard to find an address in a rural city of two thousand residents. I saw their white, plantation style home at the end of the long driveway as soon as I turned off the main road. It was a huge house—at least three thousand square feet, I'd guess, with a four-car garage attached to the house by an old-fashioned breezeway. It didn't have any trees or landscaping. I assumed the house was new and they hadn't gotten around to that yet. There was an unfurnished wrap-around porch. I rang the doorbell—not sure anyone would answer and make the whole trip a waste of time."

"What did she say when she saw you standing there?"

"Well, Carole was pleasant enough and she welcomed me in. She took one of the portraits from me and set it down against the wall in the foyer without even looking at it. I told her I left her a message to let her know I was coming and to call me back if she wasn't going to be home, and since she didn't call, I assumed it was all right. She said she appreciated me making the trip, although it really wasn't necessary, and that I could have just waited until after the estate sale, as we'd discussed." Alyx sighed.

"Judging from how you said she was dressed when you met her," I could hear Maggie say, "I'm curious as to what the inside of her house looks like."

"The living room is unfurnished as is the dining room," replied Alyx into the receiver. "The rest of the rooms I glimpsed on the way to the family room were sparsely furnished. The family room is the only room completely furnished. The transitional style furniture is tasteful and expensive. A low, decoratively painted cabinet holds a large-flat screen TV. Built in shelves flank the fireplace and showcase beautiful bound books and other *objets d'art*. The room is perfect in every detail. Carole took a seat on the couch, and I sat on the loveseat facing her. I leaned the portrait I carried along the side of the couch and asked how long she'd lived there. A little color appeared on her cheeks then. I was embarrassed for asking when she said that right after they moved in, her husband's company did some downsizing, starting with his paycheck, and they had to hold off on furnishing the rest of the house.

I asked her what kind of work her husband does and she said his company designs, sells, and installs security systems for businesses and then she quickly changed the subject."

"Did she say why she left the portraits behind?" Maggie's voice rang out.

"No, she didn't and there wasn't an appropriate place in the conversation to ask."

"How did she react when she saw them?"

"She didn't. In fact, she didn't look at them at all while I was there, which means that she knew who they were and must have left them behind intentionally. Maggie, this whole thing about Althea has me baffled. I don't understand why she was killed, and who could have hated her enough to want to kill her."

Alyx shifted the phone to the other ear and I changed position.

"Carole even admitted to me that she and Althea didn't get along. She said Althea filled her son's head with stories about the diamond hidden in the desk. Apparently, she had forgotten that her husband had burned the desk. I hope that I didn't contribute to that illusion."

"What do you mean?"

"The first time she came in the store and asked me where I got the desk, I told her what I'd been told—that it was part of an estate whose owner had lived out of the country for many years. At the time, I didn't notice anything unusual; then again, I wasn't looking for anything unusual. It wasn't until much later that she told us about her life in Africa."

"If she thought that it was the same desk why did she wait seven months to buy it?" Maggie asked.

"I wondered the same thing. Carole said I didn't know her aunt very well. She had money and could have paid for the desk when she saw it. Evidently, Althea told Carole that she could probably get the desk for half of what I was asking, if not free. By then, I had a knot in my stomach."

"I'm sorry, Alyx. I know you thought a lot of her. It sounds like she was starting to lose her grip on reality—you can't hold her responsible."

"Carole said the same thing. She said her aunt was sick and although they released her from the mental health facility where she'd lived for ten years, she was never the same. I said that I understood and that was the reason I felt compelled to find out who killed her and why. At that point, Carole got up and I took it to mean it was time for me to leave. She walked me to the door, thanked me for bringing the portraits, and shut the door before I stepped off the porch. I got in the car and saw a vehicle approaching, clouds of dust in its wake. Since the driveway wasn't wide enough for two vehicles, I waited for it to pull up. A skinny young man in baggy jeans, black t-shirt and a black cap, lumbered up to the side door without looking at me."

"Not a very friendly bunch, are they? I'm sorry the trip was such a disappointment."

"I know. I'm thinking that maybe I should forget about it and leave it for Smarts to handle."

"I'm glad to hear you say that, although I don't believe you. Did you do anything else—like shop for a ball gown?"

"On the way to Umatilla, I passed the Sand Hill Mall and thought it might be a good idea to stop on the return trip and look for a dress for the masked ball. It didn't seem like such a good idea anymore though when I pulled into the parking lot. I drove around the lot twice before I found a parking space out in the boondocks.

Inside the mall, people were aimlessly wandering around, some with shopping lists in hand, others with scowls on their faces and I couldn't wait for all the hustle and bustle to be over. Anyway, after an hour of shopping, I was ready for a break and took the escalator down to the food court. As you know, shopping has never been high on my list of favorite activities, and I always reward the effort by having something I don't normally eat, usually some greasy fried food. I remembered why I was there before it was too late, and opted for a salad instead. I finished lunch and wasted another hour not finding anything I liked.

I reached the lounge area in the middle of the mall, and stopped to listen to the string quartet playing. The musicians, in formal attire, looked bored and played well, so I decided to sit and listen for a while. I'm not a classical music fan; I didn't know the piece they were playing. I was so enthralled, I didn't move until they took a break, thirty minutes later. When I got up to leave, I saw the handsome violinist who had made eye contact with me once or twice, walking towards me. Okay, don't laugh. I was in a hurry to avoid him and I nearly ran into a decorative column that wasn't there before."

That started Maggie laughing. "I'm sorry, you're so funny when a man pays you the slightest attention, and I can't help laughing."

Alyx smiled and said, "I'm glad you think it's funny."

"So you still don't have a dress for the event of the year on New Year's Eve?"

"Yes I do. I found a dress that I think is perfect for the occasion."

Alyx described the simple elegant green satin gown that she found at a little dress shop in what used to be the downtown commercial area in Agape Beach.

"The gown sounds gorgeous. Do you know what your mask looks like?"

"No. David said he wanted to surprise me. I'm sorry that you and George can't make it. It would have been fun."

"Yeah, I know. George didn't want to tell his son to change his flight reservations, so we have to pick him up at the airport that night and, of course, we can't leave him home alone."

"Who made his reservations?"

"His son did—since he had no plans to go out. Anyway, you have fun. Have a glass or two of champagne for me, and I want to hear all about it."

"If I have fun, for sure you won't hear all about it," she joked. "Okay, now do you want to know the other reason I called?"

"Sure, why did you call?"

"Sit down if you're standing because you're going to be shocked when you hear this. Do you think your cleaning lady would be interested in another client?"

"Betty Quattelbaum would be delighted. She mentioned the other day that a client had moved away and she was looking for another. Who's interested?"

"It's me. I admit it; I'm not superwoman, and I can actually afford to pay someone to come in to do the one job I have always hated. It doesn't mean I'm lazy or pampering myself; it means I'm choosing where to direct my energy."

Maggie chuckled. "You don't have to explain or justify it to me, sweetie. I'm glad you're finally starting to put yourself first."

"It's easy to put myself first now that I'm the only one standing in line."

"Good point. Hold on, I'll get you her number."

Later, while Alyx was busy around the house, Pooky took the opportunity to sneak a few morsels from the non-diet food bowl. She understood she had special food to eat and she was not to eat the other food. Still hungry and food still in the other bowl, she sat far enough away, yet close enough to scoop out a few morsels, and casually drag each one over with her paw. Alyx saw what she was up to and allowed her to sneak another paw-full before she cleaned up the leftovers.

The day was going fine, until Alyx dragged the arch-enemy—the vacuum cleaner—out of the hall closet. I was grateful that she waited a bit before she turned it on, giving us the opportunity to run. The female cats scattered to their safe places; I stood my ground—it was personal with me. I knew it was a machine, yet something about it distressed me. I tried to fight the menace by staring it down as it came my way sucking everything in its path. I even tried to attack it—the infernal machine kept on whining, and since my housemates were in hiding, I gave up and ran for cover.

"To err is human, to purr is feline."
—Robert Byrne

CHAPTER THIRTEEN: *The Encounter*

A new year arrived along with Alyx's New Year's resolution, which was to donate most of the goodies that customers dropped in the basket to the animal shelter, which managed colonies of free-roaming, abandoned, and feral cats in the area. I think she selected that shelter because of Pooky.

Alyx made up a simple tent card and placed it next to the basket on the counter. *We thank you for your generosity and we will share with our less fortunate brothers and sisters who have no home. Thank you kindly for your continued support.* (Paw prints). *Murfy, Misty, Pooky.*

The desk was now back in the store much to Misty's chagrin; I wasn't interested in inspecting it or any of the other pieces of furniture that had come back from Althea's. On the other hand, Misty had put in a considerable amount of time inspecting the desk. Alyx saw her trying to paw open one of the small drawers and joined her. Misty watched Alyx closely as she pulled all the drawers out, checking each one.

Coming up behind Alyx, Maggie asked, "Are you looking for hidden treasure?"

"In a manner of speaking, yes, I am. I can't help but wonder if this desk had anything to do with Althea's murder."

"In what way?"

"I don't know exactly. I have a feeling about it, is all."

"I think Smarts needs more than a feeling. Never mind that; I want to know about the masked ball. How was it?"

"It started out great, and turned into the strangest experience I've ever had."

Alyx looked around. "Come on; we can talk in the workroom," she said mysteriously. I followed the two women as they talked. "David arrived promptly at seven. Oh, Maggie, he was positively gorgeous in his black tuxedo, the silver at his temples accentuating his soft blue-gray eyes. I couldn't stop smiling and laughing with pleasure when I saw the elaborate mask he'd brought me—it was gold, decorated with multi-colored feathers and doodads. We left the house laughing; our conversation on the way to the ball was light and festive. When we arrived at the Atlantic Hotel and Conference Center, the President of the Music Theater Society, who's a familiar face associated with all the elite of Beachside, was directing guests to the ballroom. I greeted her. She's an older, attractive woman and she was wearing a lovely gown, but, oh, you should have seen the gaudy diamond necklace she was wearing! She smiled at David then turned back to me and said in this snooty voice, "I do believe this is the first time I have ever seen you in something other than jeans. Alyx, you look lovely." Alyx was pretending to be the lady she was describing and she looked very funny doing her imitation. If cats could laugh, I would have.

Then she continued with her story. "David came to my defense and told the woman that I looked lovely no matter what I was wearing."

"Good for him," said Maggie.

"He put his arm around my waist and led me to our table," continued Alyx. "He asked me if I knew the woman well. I told him she considered me an enemy because I'd refused to redecorate her house when I found out that all her choices were based solely on buying the gaudiest and most expensive of everything."

"Who did you sit with?" asked Maggie.

"I didn't know any of the people sitting at our table. Except for the young couple sitting next to me, none of them seemed to be interested in knowing who I was, and that was fine with me. I did recognize some of the city's prominent citizens from their pictures in the society pages of the local paper."

"How was the dinner?" Maggie grilled her friend. "I hope at least that was good."

"Well, let me put it this way," said Alyx, "The only thing that made dinner memorable was David's attentiveness. Just before the dancing started, the evening got really weird. I trooped to the ladies room with some other ladies and out in the hallway, a woman in a Marie Antoinette costume wearing a mask grabbed me by the arm and pulled me aside."

"Who was it? What did she say?"

"I had no idea who she was. But I assumed it was David's ex-wife when she said to enjoy the evening and to remember that David was *hers* anytime she wanted him back. The inflection in her voice was unmistakable as to her intentions."

Maggie got up to refresh her coffee, and a worried expression crossed her face when she turned away from Alyx. She smelled trouble the same as I did.

"Did she say anything else?" asked Maggie.

"That was it. She turned and walked away. Melissa, the young woman I sat next to at the table was waiting for me by the door and I just followed her into the bathroom. My hand was shaking violently as I tried to apply fresh lipstick, and I had to stop before it ended up all over my chin. Melissa asked me if I knew who the woman was, and I said I sort of did and let it go at that."

"What about David? Did you tell him about the encounter?"

"I didn't mention it. I put it out of my mind and tried to enjoy the rest of the evening. David turned out to be a delightful dancer—I didn't step on his toes once," Alyx joked.

"Did you see Marie Antoinette again?"

"I saw her on the dance floor; her mask was off and her eyes were boring into David. I couldn't tell if he made eye contact with her—he must have because as soon as the music stopped, he walked me back to the table. He looked like he wanted to say something to me, but the opportunity was lost when one of his colleagues asked me to dance. So we both danced with different partners and came back to the table together. David never said a word about the woman. When midnight arrived, we all toasted with champagne. David said, 'Here's to the beginning of a new year that I hope will be filled with our happy memories.' And just as he said it, I could see Marie Antoinette staring at me from across the room, her glass raised, as David put his arms around me for the traditional New Year's Eve kiss. Some happy memory."

I held my breath as Alyx seemed to hold hers. Then she continued, "We left before the room started to empty. The ride home was quiet. I don't know if David had seen his ex-wife follow me to the restroom or the exchange between us. The goodnight kiss he gave me at the door was at best tentative. I didn't invite him in and he didn't ask."

"It's hard to believe," offered Maggie, "that David Hunter, the famous trial lawyer, would ever be at a loss for words. How do you feel about what happened?"

"Maggie, you know I like David. I don't want to get involved with someone who still has issues with his ex-wife."

"Yes, but how do you know it's his issues? Maybe it's all hers."

"Whatever the case, it's not a clean break, and I don't want to deal with it."

"Although you haven't asked," said Maggie, "I'm of the opinion that you should talk to David about it. At our age, men like him don't come along too often."

"For heaven's sake, Maggie, I'm not desperate."

"I didn't mean it like that, Alyx, and you know it."

At that moment, Nelda appeared at the door asking for help on the floor, and the girls' conversation ended there.

Later, tucked away in a secluded spot in the loft, I tried to reconnect with the diamond thief. I knew what the man looked like, knew his first name and was sure his last name wasn't *Baby* as in *"Mark, baby; you're toast."* I knew this because a few days before the diamond robbery, someone had left the back door of Antiques & Designs open, and I couldn't resist taking a walk down the alley. While I was strolling, I saw two men arguing. Actually, only one was doing the arguing, the other—much smaller in stature—was silent. In a threatening tone, the beefy man with a red bulbous nose was poking his finger hard at the other man's shoulder, his face inches away. Between clenched teeth, I heard him say, *"You got two more days to pay up, Mark, baby, or you're toast."*

At the time, I didn't have the slightest idea who the beefy man was and I still don't. However, I'm sure that the man who was threatened in the alley and the man who came into the store right after the jewelry store robbery are one and the same. I concentrated as hard as

I could to recall all I'd seen and heard in the alley, searching for the slightest clue to help me identify the thief and the determine a way to tell Alyx. In my mind's eye, I saw the man dressed in business clothes: brown slacks, white shirt, conservative striped tie, and brown shoes with tassels. When he saw me in the alley, he started acting strange; he seemed to lose interest in the other man. The altercation didn't last long. The large man drove away in his car, and the other man started walking down the alley. Out of curiosity, I followed him.

He kept looking over his shoulder, and at first, I thought he was watching for the other man, but when he started walking faster and I kept pace with him until we were both running, I realized that he was running away from me! The poor man must have had ailurophobia—fear of cats! I slowed down and he ducked in the back door of the last building on the block.

After thinking about the incident in the alley for some time, it suddenly came to me—*brown shoes with tassels and no socks*—Alyx would certainly recognize that and I started working on a plan.

"Cats always know whether people like or dislike them. They do not always care enough to do anything about it."
—Winifred Carriere

CHAPTER FOURTEEN: *What the Neighbor Saw*

Alyx and Maggie parted company after they returned from their client's home. Alyx didn't tell Maggie where she was going; only that she'd see her back at the store later. As usual, I was ready to jump in the truck. The way I figured, it wouldn't hurt to try, and she could always say no if she didn't want me along; there are always other ways to get information. Luckily, she let me tag along and we ended up at Althea's condominium.

Bill Emmett, Althea's next-door neighbor, was outside working on his little pocket of a garden, a planting area in front of his townhouse-style condominium.

"Hi, Bill. Do you remember me? I met you earlier this week. My name is Alyx," she said.

"Oh, sure, I remember you. I never forget a young, pretty face," he grinned.

"Thank you; but I'm not so young."

"When you're ninety, anything less is young." He laughed; Alyx smiled. "Brought your kitty again, I see." Alyx ignored his comment but I snuggled up between the two of them so I could hear their conversation.

"Bill, I know the police have asked you questions as to what you saw or heard the night Althea was killed. I wonder if there's anything you might have remembered since."

"Funny you should ask me that because I was discussing it with the wife the other day. She's eighty-nine; doesn't get out anymore, only for doctors' appointments, and she likes to get her hair done once a week. Someone commented on the expense of getting her hair done and I said it's cheaper in the long run if it keeps her happy, if you get my meaning."

Alyx nodded and tried to get him back on the subject. "What were you and your wife discussing?"

"Because we live on a cul-de-sac, we get a lot of people turning around when they realize they've reached the end of the street and there's no exit. I usually don't pay much attention, except the day you came by with the delivery. I happened to be looking out the kitchen window and I remember I saw a car following you. It didn't come this far; it parked in the visitor parking lot across the way," he said, pointing in that direction. "It caught my attention because no one got out of the car. My wife called to me from the couch to bring her a glass of water; she doesn't walk much anymore. You see how it is. When I went back to the kitchen and looked out the window, the car was gone. I forgot all about it until yesterday. I told Jo-Jo—that's my wife—that I should tell the police. She didn't agree because my vision isn't so good anymore, and she says maybe I was wrong."

I thought his vision might surely be good enough to see a vehicle, if not the driver. Alyx must have thought the same thing, and she asked him about the driver.

"I didn't see his face; it was hidden by some sort of cap and sunglasses."

"You said he was driving a dark sedan. Was it gray, brown, black?"

"It was a dark color is all I can tell you for sure."

"Have you given this information to the police?"

"No, because I can't swear to what I saw. My wife is right. My distance vision isn't so good anymore and my close-up vision isn't any better." He laughed again.

"Thanks for the information, Bill, and don't worry about swearing to what you saw, maybe someone else closer to where the vehicle was parked got a better look."

She declined his invitation for coffee, telling him she'd love to meet his wife another day when she wasn't pressed for time.

I wondered if anyone else had mentioned the vehicle to the police. Then again, the vehicle may not have been following them at all, simply going in the same direction.

"There are few things in life more heartwarming than to be welcomed by a cat."
—Tay Hohoff

CHAPTER FIFTEEN: *An Impromptu Lunch Invitation*

On Wednesday, shortly after we arrived at the store, Alyx received a mysterious visit from her son, Ethan.

"Hi, Mom. Can you get away for lunch?"

"I think so. What's the special occasion?" she asked suspiciously

"No special occasion. It's been a while since I took you to lunch, and I don't want you to feel like you're being neglected."

"Honey, rest assured, I don't feel neglected and I'd love to have lunch with you. Will you pick me up or do you want to meet somewhere around eleven-thirty?"

"I'll come and get you; that'll give me a chance to talk to Maggie too. I haven't seen her for several weeks. Will she be here?"

"She asked about you the other day. I know she wants to see you. I'll tell her you're coming."

"Okay, Mom, I'll see you later."

I knew Ethan well enough to know he had something else in mind besides lunch. Ecstatic to see him when he arrived later that morning, Misty and I greeted him with enthusiasm while he waited for Maggie to finish up with a customer, and he reciprocated.

"Hey, handsome!" Maggie said, giving Ethan a hug. "It's been a while."

"Not my fault. The last time I was here you were off somewhere with George and you couldn't make it when Mom invited you for dinner at her house."

"Yeah, you're right. It's great to see you. So, what's new?"

While they visited, Alyx concluded her business with a client and I stayed close to Ethan, hoping to increase my chances of tagging along.

"Another new restaurant recently opened on Pelican Street. They have outside seating and I'm sure it's all right to bring Murfy. I know he wants to go," said Ethan, apparently reading my mind.

Alyx reluctantly agreed. Ethan had traded his expensive SUV for a practical compact with a standard transmission that he said was helping him save money on gas, and he insisted on driving the short distance to the casual Greek restaurant housed in a renovated 1940s two-story building painted a silvery blue and white. Ethan asked for a table on the large outside patio. Everyone ordered the special of the day and chatted about the changes taking place on Ocean Street.

Alyx said the downtown renovation effort was finally on the move. Some spaces were still empty though, and there was grumbling from some merchants about neighborhood construction projects that seemed to have no end.

Ever since Alyx and Maggie had convinced the merchants to stay open later during the week, and had established weekend hours, the area had become more of a focal point for residents and visitors. Monthly events such as a wine festival, a street party on St. Patrick's Day, the Arts Festival, and the Rum Festival served to make downtown Beachside a fun destination. Alyx was sure that it would all be worth it in the end.

Their food arrived—some sort of eggplant dish that didn't look very appetizing to me, maybe because I hate vegetables. The authentic Greek waiter called it *moussaka*.

The conversation shifted to the real reason for the lunch date when the waiter left our table.

"Mom, you've probably guessed that I have another reason to have lunch with you," said Ethan, quickly adding, "I mean other than wanting to spend time with you."

She smiled in answer. "I figured as much. So, what's up?"

He took a deep breath. "I want to buy my own place. I think I'm ready for the responsibility, and I've been thinking about settling down."

"Have you asked Nikki to marry you?" she asked, excited at the prospect.

"No. We're not ready to get married; only to start working on it. So, here's what I want to do," he said sitting forward a little, "I want to buy a house that needs work, move in and fix it up at my leisure when I can afford it. What do you think?"

"I think it's a great idea if you're ready to make the long-term commitment and put in the hard work required."

"Yeah, I am."

"Okay then, how can I help you?"

"I could use your help talking with mortgage lenders and afterwards with the renovation itself. You know, finding some authentic stuff or good reproductions, like light fixtures and things."

"Have you looked at any places, yet?" His wide grin made her joyful. "What? What did you find?"

"You know that rundown house with the plantation style wrap-around porch on Peninsula Drive?"

When she shook her head, he continued, "The one I wanted you to buy when you were looking for a house."

"You mean the house on the river that wasn't for sale when you wanted me to buy it?"

"Yup, that's the one, only it's for sale now. The owner's in a nursing home; his family is scattered, and they don't want to fool around with it. It's on the market for one-eighty. You think it's a good price?"

"Your uncle would be the one to talk to about that. He's the real estate investor."

"Yeah, that's what Dad said, too. He offered to help with the down payment. Can you help me out if I need a co-signer?"

"I'll be glad to. I know you've learned your lesson about financial responsibility. After you get your uncle's opinion on the property and its value, I'll talk to some lenders and see who offers the best deal."

When the lunch had finally ended and the conversation too, Ethan paid the check and dropped us off in front of the store.

"I'll call Uncle Tom and see if he can look at the place today," said Ethan. "I'll let you know what he says."

"Okay, sweetheart, and thanks for lunch."

"The smart cat doesn't let on that he is."
—H. G. Frommer

CHAPTER SIXTEEN: *Murfy, the Escape Artist*

Alyx was on the phone when I wandered into the workroom. I heard her greet Ethan on speaker phone and I didn't hear a response. He went straight to the reason for his call.

She looked amused. "Take a deep breath, Ethan. I can tell you're a little excited; it's not every day you buy your first home. I've already made some calls, and the bank we do business with offers the best interest rate. Colonial Bank is at the end of our block. If you can come to the store in about an hour, we can walk over."

I realized she was talking about the building where I had seen the man arguing in the alley enter. One never knows, though I was fairly certain that Alyx wouldn't bring me with her to the bank, I patiently waited by the door for Ethan to arrive. I had been looking for a way to communicate what I knew about the man in the alley, whom I suspected was the diamond thief, and it couldn't have worked out better. My only concern was that if he did work in the bank, she wouldn't recognize him and—for that reason—it was imperative that I go with them. Also, while waiting I sent out a special call to a friend. When Ethan stuck his head in the door, Alyx grabbed her purse and followed him. Distracted by Ethan's haste, she didn't see me slide out the door on her heels. I trotted along, a cat on a mission, avoiding feet and other obstacles, careful to keep my humans in sight ahead of me.

At the end of the block, I gave Alyx and Ethan some lead time before I followed them inside the bank before the door closed. I immediately hid behind a large flowerpot near the entrance, and when the opportunity presented itself, I came out from behind it and lurked behind a uniformed woman. Now and then, I nosed the carpet, my mouth open as I took in the scent of the most-recent visitors—none of them cats. I cautiously moved forward, staying close to the wall. The doors to the offices on either side of the foyer were open with no sign of Alyx or Ethan. In the main room of the building, there were three desks on one side of the room, and one desk on the other side next to a long counter, partitioned into six spaces.

I hid under an upholstered chair up against the wall in the main area and surveyed the room. My humans sat at the first desk across the room. I could see them, but they couldn't see me. The diamond thief sat at a desk next to the counter across the room facing his computer. I noticed that he kept glancing in Alyx's direction without moving his head.

The only way he was going to stand up so Alyx could notice him was if I scared him as I had done in the alley. Unfortunately, I couldn't show myself with Alyx and Ethan in the room. Knowing that, I sent out another call to my special helper—one of Pooky's outdoor friends to help me out. His name was Zipper, a black cat—chosen for drama and speed.

Zipper had slipped into the bank after me and now was hiding under another chair. On my signal, he sprinted across the room at the speed of light, and I ran to the exit. No one was in the hallway; no one saw me leap to hit the handicap door opener.

The ruse worked. Zipper said the diamond thief (his nameplate said he was called *Merkley*) practically jumped off his chair to get out of the way, but that's all he could report. I didn't know if Alyx noticed him or even recognized him; I had to wait for her to get back to the store and then hear what she had to say.

Luckily, I left the bank unseen and returned unharmed to the store. I hoped Misty was on guard at the checkout counter. She ran to find someone to let me in when she saw me.

Alyx came back from the bank a short time later, and I followed her to the workroom.

Maggie ended her phone conversation when she saw Alyx walk in and asked, "How did it go? Is he getting the loan?"

"Yes, no problem as long as I co-sign. I can't believe my little boy is becoming a homeowner. I'm so proud of him, Maggie."

"I know you are, and you should be."

Maggie said she had an appointment with a man about reupholstering a chair, and mentioned my excursion. "By-the-way, I think Murfy had himself an exciting time while you were gone."

"What did he do now?" asked Alyx.

"I think he followed you, or tried to."

"I didn't see him get out."

Maggie shook her head and shrugged, "Well, maybe he followed a customer. All I know is that I heard Misty walking around meowing, and when she saw me, she bounded to the front door where Murfy was waiting outside. I didn't even know he was gone until I saw him waiting at the door."

Alyx looked at me suspiciously and frowned.

"Maybe this was a one-time adventure, an opportunity he couldn't resist," Maggie joked.

"I think my cat is an escape artist, only he knows all the places he's been." said Alyx, unfortunately providing me with no information about whether or not she had recognized the diamond thief at the bank.

"Cats can be cooperative when something feels good, which, to a cat, is the way everything is supposed to feel as much of the time as possible."
—Roger Caras

CHAPTER SEVENTEEN: *A Predictable Plot*

Alyx made a fresh pot of coffee, poured two cups, and brought one to Maggie along with a plate of muffins she'd picked up earlier from the Café.

"Take a break; I want to run something by you," she said, setting the coffee and muffins in front of her.

Maggie took a sip of the hot coffee, reached for a muffin and leaned back in her chair.

"Okay, I'm listening."

"Remember the nervous guy I told you about that came in the store the day Hall's was robbed?"

Maggie answered with a blank look on her face.

Alyx continued, "The one who stepped on Misty on his way out."

"Oh, yeah. You said you thought he was embarrassed because everyone was staring at him." She laughed and took a bite of the muffin in her hand.

"Well, I don't know if I mentioned it at the time but he looked familiar, and now I know why; he works at the bank, our bank. His name is Mark Merkley."

"Who?"

"Mark Merkley. The name plate on his desk said Mark Merkley."

The baffled look on Maggie's face hastened an explanation. "I saw him today when I was there with Ethan. He was dressed in a shirt and tie, wearing the same brown shoes with tassels and no socks—the same as the man who stepped on Misty the day Hall's was robbed. I didn't recognize him at the time because when he was in the shop he was dressed casually and his face was hidden by a baseball cap and sunglasses."

"Alyx, don't forget; you haven't been in the bank since Bernice started making the deposits."

"That's the truth."

"So what happened that made you look at this guy's feet?"

There was a moment of silence, and then Alyx continued. "I think he's ailurophobic; he has an irrational fear of cats."

"And how do you know that?"

"This is going to sound strange but hear me out ..." She went on to recount what I already knew had happened. Then, they both looked down at me, frowning.

"Okay, getting back to what I was saying ... here's what I'm thinking. What if he—this Mark Merkley—stole that diamond from Hall's and hid it in the desk in our shop, intending to get it later when the heat was off, except we delivered the desk to Althea. He could have been watching and saw where it went."

"And he went back later to get his diamond and killed Althea in the process," finished Maggie.

"Exactly. So you think it could have happened that way?"

"It could have, except it sounds too much like the predictable plot of a bad mystery novel."

Alyx bit her lower lip, "Yeah, I guess it does at that."

"Besides, how can you approach the police with just a theory? Don't they have to have evidence before they can investigate?"

Alyx shrugged.

"Did you let on that you recognized him when you were in the bank today?"

"Not outwardly. Don't worry I'm not going to do anything foolish. Not where that's concerned anyway. I'm going to tell Smarts about recognizing him, and about the behavior of the man who came in the store after the robbery and who I think he is. Right now, it's just speculation on my part that he killed Althea, and Smarts may come to that same conclusion. No question though, I do think he stole the diamond."

Alyx then called Detective Smarts regarding Mark Merkley, the alleged diamond thief. He asked her to come into the station to file a formal statement. I was delighted that she decided to take me along.

At the station, I expected a cool reception and wasn't disappointed. Smarts practically hissed when he saw me trailing behind Alyx.

"Why didn't you give us this information about this Merkley character earlier, Ms. Hille?"

"It didn't occur to me then."

"What made you think of it now?"

"I guess it was because of his behavior today in the bank for one. I used to make our bank deposits at least three times a week for more than two years, and he— this Merkley fellow—always said *hello*. I haven't been making the deposits recently, so I haven't been in the bank very often and therefore haven't seen him. Today when I was there with my son, and I saw him, I remembered that he had been in my store the day of the diamond robbery. Secondly, you don't usually see men in suits wearing dress shoes with no socks, and I remembered that the guy who came in the store after the robbery also wore brown shoes with tassels and no socks."

"So you think we should question him based on what you just told me."

"Look, I had information and I gave it to you. You do what you want with it." She grabbed the purse she'd slung across the back of her chair and walked out, her cheeks red.

Back at the shop, customers continued to trickle in all evening. I sat on the counter carefully monitoring the comings and goings, on the lookout for Mark Merkley.

David Hunter called for Alyx and left a message on the answering machine in the workroom. The message was the same as the one he'd left on the answering machine at home and probably on her cell phone— asking her to call him.

Alyx hesitated a moment, took a deep breath and then called him. I was close enough to hear him say he was hoping to have dinner with her and she could pick the place.

"How about dinner at my house?" she suggested, "Nothing fancy. I'll make spaghetti and a salad."

"Okay, I'll bring the wine and, Alyx…did I tell you how beautiful you looked the other night?"

Her eyes softened. "Yes, several times," she said.

The bright red-orange glow must have drawn Alyx to the screened porch. The western sky was ablaze with the setting sun. At first glance, one might have thought that the woods in the distance were on fire.

Hunter arrived promptly at six. He uncorked the wine and filled two glasses, while Alyx served a simple dinner of mixed salad greens, spaghetti with homemade tomato sauce and garlic bread sticks.

She let him do most of the talking during dinner, telling her funny stories about other masked balls and charity events he'd attended. Their conversation touched mostly on the surface of things. They finished dinner, and Hunter deposited the dirty dishes in the sink while Alyx put away the leftovers. He refilled the wine glasses and carried them to the living room. Alyx followed and sat next to him on the couch. For a moment, neither one seemed to know what to do or say.

Alyx spoke first. "David, I agreed to see you because what I have to say needs to be said in person... I think you know I'm attracted to you." He took her hand, and she pulled it back. "The relationship with your wife…"

"Ex-wife," he interjected.

"Your relationship with your ex-wife isn't over, and I don't want to be involved in a triangle."

She told him about the encounter at the ball.

"Alyx…."

She shook her head. "I'm sorry David—there can't be anything serious between us with a third party still involved."

He reached for his glass, "Joann and I have known each other since grade school; we dated exclusively in high school, and married while still in college. She's been restless for a long time. She doesn't want me—she just doesn't want anyone else to have me. Believe me, Alyx, it's over between us."

"That's just it; I don't believe it is. You have too much history between you. I'm truly sorry, but I can't deal with it."

"So, that's it, we're finished?"

"We can see each other as before."

"Yes, we can do that; see each other once or twice a month for coffee. How long do you think we can do that without giving up?"

"For me, it's until you're truly free."

There was nothing left to say. He nodded silently, his eyes dark with displeasure, maybe a little anger, surely not at her. He drained his wine and stood to leave. She walked him to the door and said goodnight. Closing the door behind her, she leaned her back against it. She turned and quickly pulled the door open expectantly but he was gone.

"A cat has absolute emotional honesty: human beings, for one reason or another, may hide their feelings, but a cat does not."
—Ernest Hemingway

CHAPTER EIGHTEEN: *One Less Suspect*

The sun streaming in the bank of windows in the kitchen warmed the chilly tile underfoot, making it comfortable enough to sit and watch Alyx eat her breakfast—a bowl of oatmeal and a handful of vitamins. It wasn't unusual for the temperature to fluctuate dramatically, and according to the weather forecast, it would rise to the low eighties by noon.

The phone rang; I jumped on the chair next to Alyx and heard Maggie's excited voice.

"Alyx, have you read the paper, yet?"

"No, I haven't. Why?"

"Mark Merkley was killed last night."

"How?" she asked, as she unfolded the paper and scanned each page until she found the article.

"Someone shot him. A neighbor heard the shot and called the police. Read the article and I'll see you at the store this afternoon."

"Okay, sweetie, thanks for calling."

By late afternoon we were all at the shop and Alyx had more information on the shooting. A neighbor of Merkley's had heard shots fired, and when he looked out the window, he saw a car pull away. He didn't get the license plate number, only the make and color of the vehicle. Other neighbors said they saw that same car parked in front of Merkley's house several times during the week, and didn't see anyone getting in or out of the car.

"I heard that the police interviewed his girlfriend," Alyx was saying to Maggie, "and she told them he was a gambler, got into a high-stakes poker game here in town, suffered a heavy loss, and borrowed money from a loan shark to pay his debt. Word on the street is that he was killed because he didn't pay them back."

"That makes sense," said Maggie. "How much did he borrow?"

"Thirty-thousand," replied Alyx, "and I don't think it's a coincidence that it's the same amount the stolen diamond was worth. I was thinking about Mark Merkley after I read the short blurb in the paper about him and the thought suddenly struck me that if he got killed because he didn't pay his gambling debts, then he didn't kill Althea for sure."

"So you're thinking the diamond must still be in the desk, if that's where he hid it."

The women trotted out the door before Maggie finished her sentence, and I trotted over to Misty. I asked her to guide Alyx to where she saw the thief hide the diamond, and she was thrilled to lead the parade.

Alyx, however, didn't make it to the desk. A round, pasty-faced, man with thick, red hands stopped her.

In a booming voice, he asked if she worked there. "Yes, I do. How may I help you?"

"I'm looking for an old desk that has lots of cubby holes to hide stuff. You know what I'm talking about?"

It was clear to me that Alyx had no intention of selling the desk, so she'd placed it in an out-of-the way spot in the shop, up against a wall, not easily seen unless you were looking for it.

"I know what you're looking for," Alyx said to the man, "but we don't have it. There are two other antique stores down the street, you might try there."

"A friend of mine said she saw it here the other day," he insisted.

"I'm sorry; the desk she saw is not for sale," she said as she edged away.

His face turned red, sweat appeared on his brow. "I'll pay whatever you want. The desk is for my wife. It would mean a lot to her."

"I'm really sorry; it's not for sale."

"Look, you don't understand; I did something I won't be forgiven for unless I make it up to her big. I need to buy that desk," he pleaded.

Alyx shook her head, and she repeated firmly, "It's not for sale."

"*Fine*. See if I ever come here again. And I promise, neither will anyone else I know."

He said that last part loud enough for everyone to hear, and then stomped out of the store.

"I hope he keeps his promise about not coming back, and if his friends are anything like him, I won't miss them either," said Maggie.

After the man left, Alyx took all the drawers out of the desk and kept shooing Misty away. The little cat rose on her hind legs, and kept pawing at one gaping hole, squeaking out meow after meow.

"Misty, what is the matter with you? Do you see something I'm not seeing?"

Misty answered with a loud frustrated meow and stepped aside. I stretched as tall as I could on my hind legs, stuck my paw in the first drawer space, and found the wad of gum stuck on the underside of the top, the diamond still embedded. With a quick scratch from my claws, the little gum-encrusted gem was released into Alyx's hands.

Two hours later, Alyx handed the plastic bag containing the diamond to Smarts, and he pocketed it.

"Thank you for your efforts, Ms. Hille."

"As I tried to tell you before, I thought Merkley stole it and hid it in the desk. However, I don't know that I would have ever found it if my cats hadn't insisted."

"You're too modest, Ms. Hille. Didn't you try to give your cats credit for solving the case last spring?"

"Okay, maybe they didn't solve the case, but they helped."

Standing close by, Maggie pulled her away. "Looks like you were right."

Alyx stole a glance at the departing detective, "I was right about Merkley stealing the diamond—not about killing Althea. Speaking of which—do you want to go to her place and start to price the items for the estate sale?"

"I thought we weren't going to do that, yet. Never mind, I get it. You want to snoop around some more, don't you?"

"Someone killed Althea, and he's still out there. Maybe the two of us can find a clue or something that will motivate Detective Smarts to investigate further."

"When do you want to go?"

"Since both Bernice and Nelda are working today, now seems like a good time. Do you have anything going on?"

"I have a couple of calls to make first and then I'll be ready."

I thought it would be a good idea to go along with them, so I quickly slipped out behind Maggie, and wedged myself under her seat before she could grab me. I'd used this method before with success.

While Maggie and Alyx priced the items in the kitchen cabinets to sell-on-site, I explored the area. I knew where Alyx had found Althea's body and started there.

When I'd asked Simon if he knew who'd killed his human, he said that when he'd arrived on the scene, Althea was already dead. Although my sense of smell isn't as good as the canine species, it hasn't failed me so far. As I sniffed and pawed around, I detected the scent of more than one person, and pieces of my conversation with Simon started to fall into place.

Maggie moved to the living room, and Alyx went upstairs to the bedrooms. I followed Alyx, curled up in a corner of the room and mulled over what Simon had said he'd overheard.

"You have more money than you can possibly use up before you die; why won't you help Dad?"

"Because he thinks I'm crazy and told your mother to have me declared incompetent. He could have asked me for help, instead he wants to take it all away."

Althea had never spoken badly of Carole; in fact, she hardly mentioned her at all except for the comment she made to Alyx a while back while discussing antiques. Althea said that not everyone appreciated antiques. Her niece and her husband for example, only appreciated them for their resale value. Then she added that the only thing Carole and her husband had in common was their bad temper after he took a cut in pay in order to keep his job.

We were in the large and bare master bedroom. The centerpiece of the room—the three-quarter size, circa 1880, Victorian bed with walnut and mahogany spindles, and elegantly carved roses and leaves, was for sale in Antiques & Designs. Also gone were the mahogany dresser and the Victorian lady's sitting chair, with delicately carved flowers on the curved back and an embroidered seat. The only items left were the mattress set, a laminate end table, and a mahogany painted lingerie chest.

Alyx pulled out the top drawer of the lingerie chest, carried it to the mattress, and started sorting the items into four piles. Maggie joined her when she pulled out the second drawer.

"I'm all done downstairs. How about you, did you find anything interesting?"

Alyx pointed to the pile of pictures. "Can you believe that Althea wouldn't have a picture of her child? In fact, there's no evidence in any of this stuff that a child ever existed."

"Maybe her husband got rid of everything to make it easier for her. She never mentioned having a child, so maybe she blocked it all out of her mind."

"I don't know, Maggie. You might be right. It just doesn't seem normal."

"Well, that's it from what you've told me, she wasn't."

Something caught Alyx's attention.

"Look at this, Maggie," she said, handing her the two sheets of paper. It's from the same bank we do business with and look at the balance—a whopping half-million dollars, plus or minus a few thousand, and if you add the balance from this other bank, she's worth three-quarters of a million dollars!"

Maggie's eyes widened. "You've got to be kidding! Are these statements current?" She flipped through them and answered her own question, "The one from Colonial Bank is, and so is the one from the other bank. Althea could have bought our whole inventory and the building."

She saw the look on Alyx's face and quickly added, "Oh, she had me fooled too. She seemed so lonely. Maybe she thought she needed an excuse to keep coming around."

"What do you mean?"

"Oh, you know. She said she couldn't afford to pay for the desk, so she developed a relationship with us while she supposedly saved up for it."

"Sure. That's probably how it was."

I moseyed on over to inspect the open drawer on the slim chest, and as I approached I saw the corner of an envelope sticking out from beneath the chest. I grabbed it with my teeth, gave it a tug or two, and carried it to Alyx.

"Good cat," she said, stroking my head. She turned the envelope over and read the return address aloud. "Franklin International Investigations, Inc."

Maggie cleared a spot on the mattress and sat down. I did the same without clearing a spot. Alyx opened the unsealed envelope, took out a single sheet of paper, and scanned the contents.

"Well, what does it say?"

"As incredible as it sounds—Althea's son is alive and wants to see her! Apparently, she hasn't responded to phone calls, prompting the agency to write, advising her that he plans to call on her unless they hear from her."

Alyx looked at the envelope again. "This firm is in Chicago. I wonder if that's where he lives."

"Do you think he's down here and knows she's dead?"

"The date on the letter is three weeks ago, so it's possible."

"There are no ordinary cats."
—Colette

CHAPTER NINETEEN: *The Talkative Elderly*

Alyx, Maggie, and I sat in the lobby of the police station, waiting for Smarts, and when he appeared, he was so pleasant I almost forgot I didn't like him.

"I'm sorry I kept you waiting; I had a report to finish that was due to the division chief today. So what can I do for you?"

"As you know," Alyx began, "Althea Burns's niece asked Antiques & Designs to conduct an estate sale of her things. Maggie and I went over there to prepare for the sale and found this letter among her personal items." She reached into her purse and pulled out her phone. "I didn't want to be arrested for removing evidence, so I took a picture of the letter."

She handed him the phone and asked, "Do you think her son might have been involved in her death?"

Smarts' face registered as much surprise as did Maggie's. His eyebrows shot up at the question, "There's nothing pointing to him as a suspect. Do you know something we don't?"

"Only this—there was no evidence that Althea had ever had a child and she never mentioned it to me or Maggie. According to that letter, it sounds like she's reluctant to even acknowledge her son's existence, let alone see him."

"Yes, so?"

"Maybe he went to see her and for whatever reason, she didn't believe him."

"And you think he killed her," he finished.

"Well, stranger things have happened."

"Thanks for the information. If there's anything else, Ms. Hille, I know where to reach you."

He started to walk away and turned back. "By the way, we found Mark Merkley's DNA on the gum."

"I knew you would. What puzzles me is how did he know he'd find the correct size and shape diamond he needed?"

"Mr. Hall told us that the elderly customer who sold him the diamond had applied and been denied a loan at the bank where Merkley worked. We spoke to her, and she didn't remember telling anyone at the bank about the diamond she'd sold. However, another employee saw her sitting at Merkley's desk the day she made the deposit, so it's possible that he got all the information he needed."

"Sadly, there's always someone ready to take advantage of the talkative elderly who are ready to divulge personal information to complete strangers just for the pleasure of the exchange," said Maggie. "What I don't understand is why he didn't come back to get his diamond after going through the trouble of stealing it."

"His girlfriend said that to the best of her knowledge, he'd never done anything like that before, insisting he wasn't a criminal and blamed herself for what happened."

"Why did she blame herself?"

"She told him she didn't want to get married until they could afford the down payment on a house. She jokingly suggested going to Biloxi, to seek their down payment. He did, and discovered his weakness for gambling."

On the way back to the store, Alyx asked Maggie if what she'd said about Althea's son made sense to her.

"Oh, Alyx, you know I don't have those kinds of instincts," she answered.

Alyx persisted, "Well, doesn't it make sense?"

"Yes, it does. So did the idea that Mark Merkley killed her, but that didn't happen."

They didn't have much to say to each other after that. We pulled up in the parking lot behind the store and went inside. Maggie saw that there were several customers waiting for assistance and both Alyx and Maggie pitched in. When the mini-rush ended, Alyx went back to the workroom.

Liza Sherman, a neighbor and regular customer poked her head in the door, "Hi, Alyx, got a minute?"

Liza, also known as the *Queen of Volunteers,* because she was president or vice-president of every volunteer committee in the community, could gather a force of volunteers with a snap of her fingers.

"Sure, come on in. Today's the big game for the soccer team, isn't it?"

"It is, but Lindsey won't be playing."

"Why, what happened? She was so excited about it the other day."

"She found out the playing field sits on top of a used-to-be cemetery."

"Is that true?"

"It's true all right. The City Commission decided to remember the nameless dead buried there by putting up a plaque at the entrance to the park. The kids would have probably not noticed it; but the adults did and started talking about it. When Lindsey heard, she announced that she wasn't going to play on top of dead people, and that was that."

"I can't say that I blame her," said Alyx, commiserating.

"Yeah, I don't either. I didn't try real hard to change her mind."

"How did the whole cemetery thing come about?"

"I guess the City learned about its existence some years back, and by that time, the cemetery was overgrown, there was nothing left to identify the graves and no known relatives. Since there were no laws back then about cemeteries, the City turned it into a park. A few months ago, area historians and the local cemetery preservationists brought it up to the commissioners and they decided on a plaque."

"I wonder how many more abandoned cemeteries have been built on," mused Alyx.

"I read an article," said Liza, "that said there are currently five cemeteries in the county not being maintained and may disappear. In fact, one of them is a couple of miles from here, beach side."

"I've heard it called the Rich and Poor Cemetery and the Saints and Sinners Cemetery," said Alyx.

"Why did they call it that?"

"The first one is self-explanatory and for the Saints and Sinners, I've heard it said that the church members were buried in one section and non-members in another and you can guess which was which," Alyx explained.

"Isn't it funny how we never think about some things, like cemeteries, until something happens. There's all this information that comes out, and then we forget all about it again."

That simple fact of life underscored, they switched the subject to redecorating around Liza's pool.

Alyx and Maggie had met while taking classes at the local community college. Maggie had no living family. Alyx had brothers and sisters, but her family had drifted apart after her mother's death, and no one was closer to her than Maggie was, but that didn't mean that they never argued or disagreed.

"Have you heard from David since you put your relationship on hold?" Maggie asked.

"Yes, he called and asked me to meet him for lunch. I said no at first, and then talking to him made me realize how well he filled a void I didn't know existed until recently."

"So did you meet him?" Maggie kept prodding.

"I did and I'm not sure I should have. It complicates things even more."

"Sometimes emotions overtake logic and, let's face it; relationships can get difficult."

"We had lunch at The Pier, on the south edge of Beachside. It's been a while since I was in that area and with a new subdivision going up—a strip shopping center and a business park—I almost didn't find the restaurant. It was small, intimate and dark with only two other couples seated. I wanted to leave, hesitated, and then it was too late. My eyes adjusted to the dark and I saw David, thankful that he wasn't sitting in a booth. He waited for me to approach, pulled out my chair, and took a seat across the table. He said he wanted one more chance at convincing me not to stop seeing him."

"And?"

Alyx looked away, and when she spoke, it sounded as if she was talking to herself. "This feeling has been there from the beginning and has grown over the months we've known each other. What are the chances it will happen again? Except ... I don't want to share him; I want him completely free—no attachments, all or nothing."

"Okay, so what are you saying? Have you changed your mind about seeing him?" Maggie was trying to help Alyx make up her obviously conflicted mind.

"I told him I'd consider it," she snapped. "I know your feelings on the subject, so you needn't tell me again."

"I wasn't going to do that. You're a big girl and more than capable of messing up your own life." Maggie yanked her purse from the desk, said she had an errand to run and didn't know when she'd be back.

Bernice came in a few minutes later with a message from Maggie.

"Maggie said she forgot to tell you that Annie Kron called about the chair that was delivered today and you need to call her back."

"Did she say anything else?"

"She said to be sure to tell you she's not mad at you for snapping at her and she'll see you tomorrow."

"Cats are connoisseurs of comfort."
—James Herriot, *James Herriot's Cat Stories*

CHAPTER TWENTY: *Who Is Harassing Alyx?*

Alyx stomped into the workroom with a scowl on her face. Maggie raised her head, put her pencil down, and leaned back in her chair.

"What happened this time?"

"Let's make a business decision right now to never accept a job based solely on the profit margin."

"If I remember correctly, and I do; it was your decision to take her as a client," Maggie countered.

Alyx set aside her design board and briefcase. "I need a cup of coffee. Want some?"

Maggie lifted her cup for a refill. Alyx topped it off and filled her mug with the rest, took a sip of the hot, dark liquid and sat at the worktable, stretching her legs out in front.

"She didn't like anything we put together."

"What …? We gave her exactly what she wanted."

"You know what she said? We're the designers; we shouldn't have listened to her."

Maggie—blonde hair, blue eyes, and the same age as Alyx—smiled broadly and between sips of coffee, said, "So, our plan worked."

"I resent having to play these silly games, and today I let her disrespectful attitude get to me. You and I have accomplished a lot on our own. It's difficult when a woman like her, someone who's never worked a day in her life, someone who's had everything handed to her and lives in a million-dollar home, someone with extremely bad taste…" and they burst into laughter.

They quieted down when George walked in, greeted Alyx and gave Maggie a quick kiss on the cheek. Then Alyx proceeded to tell him why they were laughing.

"Just so you don't get it wrong, I don't often do that, but in this case our reputation was at stake. Sometimes I really miss the days when it was all about the hunt, picking through old discarded things and finding that one item of value that would be sold in our store."

"Sad to say, we don't do much of that anymore," added Maggie.

"You don't have to do that anymore with so many people bringing their stuff to you," he answered. "However, if you ladies want to get back to the real thing, take a look out the window at the treasures I found at a house they're tearing down."

"No doubt to make room for another condominium," Maggie said.

"Right you are, sweetie," he said, draping his arm around her shoulders, "and these start at only five hundred thousand."

"Those cheap ones must be the ones facing the road rather than the ocean," she answered, shaking her head in disbelief.

The three of them trooped to the front of the store. George grinned at their gleeful reaction to the truckload of architectural items, along with a bathtub and a pedestal sink in pristine condition.

"George, this is perfect for the house Ethan is buying," said Alyx.

"Thank you, honey," said Maggie.

"Of course, I intent to make a small profit on this," he said, winking at Maggie.

"Fair enough, George," replied Alyx. "Wait until I tell Ethan; I know he'll be positively thrilled!"

"Do you think he'd be interested in some wood flooring? Most of it's rotted away, but there's probably just enough to salvage for a couple of rooms," said George.

"I'm sure he'll want it," said Alyx.

"If he does want it, tell him we need to get it real soon. I'll help, but we could use one more man."

"Okay, George," said Alyx, "I'll have him call you, and—thank you for thinking of him."

It was only seven o'clock when we left the store, but it was pitch-dark outside. Alyx closed all the blinds and checked all the locks on the doors again. When we got home, she prepared her tea, and while the tea steeped, she changed into an oversized t-shirt. In my opinion, it was too early to call it a night; conversely, it was not time to go out or start anything new.

Alyx called her brother Tom, told him about the items that George had picked up for Ethan, and how excited Ethan was to start the renovation process on his house.

"I've already told Ethan not to hesitate to call me for help if a job gets to be more than he can handle," said Tom. "I know contractors who will quote him a fair price."

"Thanks, Tom. I'll see you and Susan for dinner on Wednesday."

"Was there something else, Alyx?"

"Well ...no, nothing that can't wait. Good night, Tom."

She disconnected without mentioning to her brother that someone had followed us home and had almost sideswiped her car when she turned in the driveway. At first, I thought maybe Alyx had made someone mad because she was driving too slowly. However, I started to doubt that that was the case when the phone rang three different times during the night, and there was no one talking on the other end.

Trying to sleep with the phone ringing at all hours of the night was an exercise in futility. I figured someone was obviously harassing Alyx. That sideswipe was a near miss. Who could be stalking Alyx? Was it Althea's killer or was it someone else? I remembered Alyx's conversation with David about his ex-wife and considered the probability that she was the culprit.

Someone wanted to scare Alyx—at least, this time. Maybe next time, it would be worse. Either way, Pooky and Misty needed to know. When I told them, they looked at each other in alarm and then back at me. Pooky hoped her presence wasn't required at Antiques & Designs. I understood her reluctance to go. She'd learned that for superstitious reasons some humans don't like black cats; some people visibly cringed when they saw her. There wasn't much I could say about that. Malevolence wasn't new to her; she'd had some experience with that before. She plopped down with obvious relief when I told her that Misty and I could handle things for the time being.

Pooky and Misty then joined Alyx in her bedroom, and I took a watchful position at the front door where the bare sidelights provided a good view of the front yard and street. I looked carefully up and down the street as far as I could see, and there were no parked cars, moving vehicles or criminals lurking in the bushes.

Misty hadn't said a word to me since the last time she'd seen me leave the house; her quiet behavior reflected the deep disappointment she must have felt. She'd believed me when I told her I wasn't going to join Simon. Now she apparently wasn't sure. She would have been terrified had she known my inner conflict.

"Prowling his own quiet backyard or asleep by the fire,
he is still only a whisker away from the wilds."
—Jean Burden

CHAPTER TWENTY-ONE: *Do Civilized Cats Eat Rats?*

Simon was late. It was two o'clock in the morning, and I paced across the screened porch, ears forward, alert to his approach. I caught a glimpse of Misty in my peripheral vision and pretended I didn't see her.

When Simon finally appeared, I jumped through the slit in the screen and we were off, over the picket fence, across the front of the house and down the street to our meeting place. I knew Misty was following us at a discreet distance, ducking behind trees and shrubs. Every now and then, she stopped and looked around to get her bearings. Misty, an indoor cat her whole life had never expressed a desire to run free outside, yet there she was, trudging across manicured lawns, un-kept lawns, natural landscapes, and open areas. If it weren't for Simon urging me on, I would have marched her back home to safety.

Misty was familiar with most of the nocturnal animals that lived in the area—owls, snapping and gopher turtles, mice, raccoons, armadillos and an occasional opossum—only from a distance. The opossum—on a collision course with her—didn't "play dead" as I'd once told her they did, and I saw why. The mother opossum, carrying several babies on her back, bared all fifty of her teeth while making some very ugly sounds. Misty wisely gave her a wide berth with only a furtive sidelong glance.

Sounds and smells filled the night. I sensed more than saw something scurry in the tall grass in the open field. I was tempted to pounce on the rat, the primal urge stronger than I'd ever felt, and I wondered—eating a lizard was one thing—but a big rat? Do civilized cats eat rats? Truth is, there was a time when I couldn't even eat a mouse.

The house where I was born had many cracks where tiny mice made their way inside, especially under the kitchen sink. Although, he had never found any, the man of the house was always concerned about the damage a large mouse could do. On the other hand, I saw the damage he did with his old-fashioned wood traps that tortured the adult mice to death, and the poison pellets that killed them slowly.

A week before I left this home, I was exploring my surroundings and wandered into the kitchen where I found two very small creatures huddled on the floor near the baseboard. I went to inspect and called attention to the weak and vulnerable tiny mice.

In one swoop, the woman of the house grabbed the stronger one first, then the weaker one who tried to make a pitiful getaway. She placed them in a shoebox with a washcloth for comfort, birdseed, and water. She hid the box in the furnace room out of harm's way when she heard her husband come in. The tiny mice didn't notice the food or didn't know what it was, but they did seek warmth under the washcloth. I knew that they were still nursing and too young for solid food.

The woman came back later and tried to feed them milk, using her finger as a dropper. The weaker one didn't respond. The other one turned on his back and took a drop, then went back under the washcloth. I understood there wasn't anything I could do, other than let them know, they weren't alone. The weaker mouse died during the night and the other one died the next day. The woman wrapped the mice together in a piece of cloth and buried them in the pet cemetery, under the bushes by the patio wall.

The way I saw it, the mother of the baby mice probably entered the house to give birth and she lost her life when she went looking for food; there's no telling how long the babies had been there without food. I believe that when the time was right, she would have led her babies out of the house and taught them the skills they needed to survive and no one would have died.

As a kitten, every creature I met was my friend, and the death of the little mice taught me that all life deserves respect. As an adult, I'm well fed and I have no need to hunt. However, nature being what it is, I have those urges, but unless it's a matter of survival, it's up to me to decide whether to act on them or not.

Now, the trail that Simon and I were following led to a clearing—an empty lot, actually. The only thing on the overgrown property was a decaying shed at the rear of the property. We slipped through an opening in the door and disappeared inside. Another two sleek Siamese cats came through the opening and—following them—an additional two cats.

I hoped Misty had found a good listening spot, and a few minutes later, I saw her half-hidden by a wild grapevine that covered most of the shed. Simon was aware of her presence and wanted to scare her into returning home. However, I assured him that she was no threat. Inside the shed, all the cats formed a circle. I sat next to Simon, and even though I felt uncomfortable, I made no move to leave.

Sometime later, I made my way back to the house with Simon's last words firmly embedded in my brain. *"There are thousands of us roaming the country—the world, in fact. Join us and I will teach you things you never thought possible. Together, you and I can make a difference for the good of all humankind."*

The seduction was subtle, the lure of power intoxicating. As I ambled along, I mulled over the events of the night, my mind flirting with the idea of freely wandering wherever I wished, the possibilities endless. An owl hooted in the distance; a small mammal skittered nearby, filling the space around me with harmony and peace. What Simon proposed was enticing—roaming for the good of all humankind, deciding for ourselves what to do, whom to help. The question was did he mean it? Was he really interested in helping others? I told myself that if I joined him, I would make sure that's what we did.

I caught up with Misty, who'd left a few minutes before I did, running as fast as her short legs would let her, any sign of clumsiness gone, quite at home in the dark overgrown jungle. I was glad that Misty had overheard our conversation, because it would make it easier on her if I decided to leave. I could only imagine what she was thinking when she realized I was considering it.

Although, Misty had shown a great deal of courage, her sudden, loud scream was alarming. My first thought was will she remember the self-defense maneuvers I'd taught her when I'd attacked her when we were playing? I'd never really hurt her … and I was worried. When I caught up with her, a young female cat with razor sharp claws and battle scars had her up against the fence in the rear of the yard. Misty, her fur puffed out, her pupils huge in her small furry face looked fierce, determined, and fearless as she loudly told the other cat to back off, or she'd be sorry. Pooky arrived at the same time I did, and when the young female saw us all take a stand next to Misty; she knew to look for an escape route. Cat protocol dictated that she back up slowly and, once at a safe distance, she ran, tail low.

Misty was one furious fur-ball as we trotted to the safety of home, all the while asserting that she could have taken care of herself.

"I have noticed that what cats most appreciate in a human being is not the ability to produce food which they take for granted—but his or her entertainment value."
—Geoffrey Household

CHAPTER TWENTY-TWO: *The Artist*

The practice began with Alyx and Maggie dropping in at the Café for coffee and muffins-to-go before they opened the door to Antiques & Designs. Novie, the owner, told them they were welcome to come in before she opened to the public and stay for as long as they wanted. Later, she extended the invitation to other Ocean Street merchants.

While she waited for her coffee, Georgia Hamilton, owner of The Chandlery joined Alyx at the counter, with money and check in hand.

"Hi, Alyx, running late this morning?"

"Yes, we all have one of those mornings once in a while, don't we?"

"I have one of those mornings every other day."

Georgia had one of those infectious laughs that people couldn't ignore.

"What's new in your neck of the woods?" Alyx asked.

"Not much happening in my candle world, though I did hear something that might interest you."

The cashier placed Alyx's coffee on the counter and Alyx removed a couple of dollars from her wallet to pay for it. She and Georgia waited for their change, and then walked out together with me in tow.

"So what did you hear that I might want to know?" queried Alyx.

"A friend of mine who owns a collectible and antique store in Miami told me that last week an American Indian woman came into her store and asked if she was interested in purchasing some hand-crafted jewelry that she said she'd picked up for half-price from someone who wanted out of the business. When my friend took a close look at the jewelry, she noticed that some of the pieces were exactly alike—not something you see in handmade items."

"What did your friend do?"

"She told her to come back the following day; of course, she never showed up. In the meantime, my friend looked up information on the Internet and learned that there are a lot of supposedly handmade Indian articles being sold to unsuspecting tourists that are actually mass produced overseas."

"That's not a crime, is it?"

"No, as long as the item indicates the country of origin; it's only a scam when an item is said to be "authentic" Indian made. Then it becomes a federal crime, and the penalty for that can go up to two hundred-fifty thousand dollars in fines, and five years in prison."

Alyx shook her head in disbelief, "Thanks for the information. That's something that I haven't encountered so far."

"Thankfully, I don't have to worry about that in my business, but it could affect me personally. I'm wondering now, if the Amish quilt I bought for eight hundred dollars was really made by the Amish—or someone in China."

"If you like it, I don't think it matters."

Alyx saw Mary Zenn patiently waiting for her at her shop and took a couple of steps backwards, "Have a good day, Georgia," she said and hurried to her front door.

Mary fit the clichéd description of an artist with curly blond hair sticking out in all directions, running shoes that looked too big for her feet and wearing the same style (an oversized dress) that she'd worn when Alyx first met her at the Arts Festival on Ocean Street. I remember their meeting then.

Mary's booth had a simple display of only three framed pieces of artwork on their own homemade easels. The covered card table offered two more samples, and several canvases were casually leaning on either side of the table.

Mary had greeted her with a shy smile and no sales pitch. Alyx had stood back and taken a critical look at the three paintings.

"Your artwork is different than the other abstract art I've seen today."

"In the art world, this is called Abstract Expressionism. The artist expresses his state of mind with the intention of evoking an emotional chord in the viewer."

"The colors you used reflect such a serene state of mind that I can actually feel myself relaxing as I look at it."

"You have an artistic eye. These pieces are a kind of Abstract Expressionism called Chromatic Abstraction which focuses on the emotional resonance of color."

Alyx introduced herself. "My friend Maggie and I own Antiques & Designs, a couple of blocks down the street," she said, indicating the direction of the store.

"Glad to meet you, Alyx. I'm Mary Zenn. I've stopped in your store a couple of times. I really like your retro stuff and the way you display it."

"I take it you're from this area, then?"

"Yes, I live in Grand Oaks Apartments."

"I know the place. I love the large windows, and I imagine you do too."

"Yes, I do. My apartment faces west; I have a great view of the marsh, and it's all very inspiring, especially the sunsets."

Alyx looked at the scanty display of artwork and asked if she'd been painting long.

"I've been painting since I was five years old; this is my first art show."

"I take it you have more artwork at home?"

"Oh, yes. This being my first time, I wasn't sure how much to bring with me, and it looks like I was right. I've only sold a couple of pieces, and both buyers were from out of state."

"Mary, I really like your work, and I have an idea that might benefit both of us."

Mary replied with an enthusiastic nod when Alyx asked her if she wanted to display some of her art at Antiques & Designs.

"Great!" replied Alyx. "Bring it in anytime. I'll let everyone know to expect you."

The next day, Mary had arrived with five pieces of her work. Alyx was alone in the store, and they worked together to pick a spot for the display. At first, she had trouble selling anything, but now she was selling one or two pieces a month. Alyx kept encouraging her by saying that not everybody appreciated old things either, yet she was still in business and more successful every day.

We arrived now at the shop and Alyx greeted the young artist as Mary reached down to pat my head. "Hi Mary, I'm glad you're here. I have a check for you."

"And I have a painting for you."

As soon as we entered, Mary's eyes immediately went to the wall behind the counter to see if anyone had purchased her artwork.

"Who bought it, do you know?" She always asked that because, as she explained, it was important to her to know if members of her community appreciated her art.

"Someone from Palm Beach bought the blue-green piece and two other smaller pieces. He also took your card. Looks like you might get more business from him in the future. Maggie said he was very interested in knowing more about you—the artist."

"Oh, well, at least it's a Floridian, if not a Beachsider."

The check was for one hundred dollars more than the price marked.

"Alyx, there must be a mistake," said Mary looking at the check. "This is way more than what I expected."

"Well, when Maggie saw the interest in the man's face, she decided to ask for more. Frankly, we both thought they were worth more than what you marked. She said he didn't hesitate. I hope you're not mad that she took the liberty to do that."

"No, of course not. You're the one who forced me to put a price on them. I was willing for you to price them in the first place, remember?"

"Yes, and I remember telling you that if you didn't value your work, no one else would either."

"You're right; I don't have enough confidence … I'm getting better … watch!" To prove it, she folded the check with a flourish and put it in her purse without further discussion. "Well, here's the latest." She held up the canvas. The piece was larger than the others, and it had lots of color. Alyx looked for a price tag and didn't find one. "How much?"

"Well, I was going to ask you what you thought."

"What do you think its worth, Mary?"

She lifted her shoulders and squared her chin a smidgen. "I think it's worth three hundred dollars."

Alyx raised her eyebrows and said, "That might be too confident a price."

"Okay, two hundred, and not a penny less."

"You're the artist. Two hundred dollars it is."

"Yes, I am, aren't I? Shall I hang it up or will you?" she asked without hesitation.

"You do it, that way you can rearrange the pieces however you want."

The canvas was soon up and Alyx stood back. "Mary, I think this is a winner—it's absolutely beautiful," she said in awe. "I love the luminescent colors."

"What's on the canvas is not a real picture; the rectangles with the softened edges in shades of blue and white are whatever the beholder wants it to be," Mary added.

Alyx couldn't hide her emotions when Mary hugged her and thanked her for her support. She said her family didn't understand her kind of art, and had never encouraged her or shown any interest in her work, and at times, they had even acted as if her art was an embarrassment to them.

"I predict wonderful things will start happening to you soon, and I'm glad for the small part I played."

Later in the day, Alyx and Maggie were gone. Misty decided to risk another rebuff, and slid through the partially open door, stopping halfway through. I invited her in, and she entered without looking at me, skirting the outer edge of the room before she took a seat on the worktable. I joined her there, scattering a few fabric swatches in the process as I paced on the long worktable.

I owed Misty an apology for ignoring her and for hurting her feelings. I explained that I needed to set everything aside for a while.

My apology wasn't enough for Misty, however. She questioned why Simon didn't tell me who had killed Althea. I told her that I had asked Simon that question; and that his answer was that he wasn't around when it happened. Misty angrily spit out that he must have been out prowling with his friends to see how many more cats he could get to join him on his mission of good. I was stunned and I turned, facing her. Her head jerked up to look at me. She had figured out that I was considering joining Simon and she hesitantly asked when I planned to go.

Misty, and I had a special relationship; our bond had formed on that first day that Alyx had brought her home from a garage sale that included a box of free kittens. Misty depends on me to teach her and to explain things she doesn't understand; she'd be lost without me. I knew at that moment what I'd known all along—I wasn't leaving.

I didn't understand why Simon, with all his knowledge, seemed to be a little envious of me. I wondered, but only for a second, how he would react when I told him I wouldn't be joining him. The truth was that I'd known all along that my place was with Alyx.

Ready for a snack now, Misty, and I made our way to the basket of goodies on the checkout counter, disappointed at the meager supply, and there we sat patiently waiting for someone to come along and dispense the tasty treats before they all disappeared.

"The pull of the outside world is strong; there is also a pull towards the human. The cat may disappear on its own errands, but sooner or later, it returns once again for a little while, to greet us with its own type of love. Independent as they are, cats find more than pleasure in our company."
—Lloyd Alexander

CHAPTER TWENTY-THREE: *Three Is One Too Many*

"Alyx, this is David. Please call me when you get this message." Alyx put her phone down without returning the call.

Maggie plopped down on the Victorian-style couch in the workroom and asked why she was pouting.

"It's David. He left a message for me to call."

"So what's the problem?"

"I don't know if I should."

She told Maggie she didn't know what to say to him. She hadn't changed her mind about their relationship and he could be so persuasive She didn't trust herself.

"Maggie, am I crazy? He's handsome, successful, charming, kind..."

"And the cats like him," added Maggie, her best argument yet. "What else could you ask for in a man?"

Alyx leaned back in her chair and studied her nails. "Right. I'll call him."

She called his office and his assistant answered. "Dorinda, this is Alyx. David left a message to call him back. Is he available?"

"Hi, Alyx. No, he's not here. He said if you called, I was to let him know immediately, so he could call you right back."

"That's not necessary. Please just tell him that I called the next time you speak to him." I could tell that Alyx was thinking hard about something. Then she seemed to make up her mind and spoke up.

"Maggie, I'm going back to Althea's place. I won't be gone long."

Maggie didn't look up. "What are you going to do?"

"I want to take another look around, see if I missed anything."

"Be careful, Alyx. Someone may be after something in that house."

"I've thought about that; that's why I have to get there first. Besides, I don't think anyone would be stupid enough to come back in bright daylight."

"Well, they could be watching and know you're involving yourself and possibly think that you might have found something to incriminate them," Maggie argued.

"Maggie, I know you can't help being concerned, but please stop playing my mother, and stop worrying about me. I'll be careful. Nothing is going to happen to me."

"Stop playing your mother? I'm four months younger than you, and don't you forget it."

"You won't let me forget that, will you?."

"Seriously, Alyx, do you want company? I have a couple of free hours."

"No, thank you. I'll see you later." Alyx grabbed her purse and was out the back door in a flash.

I had also wanted to return to the condominium, and this was my opportunity. I surreptitiously followed her out. I saw the tailgate down and so I leaped into the truck bed. She focused on her mission, and only took a cursory look around for me. I hunched down in the corner of the truck bed, behind a rolled up rug and hoped the ride wouldn't be too rough.

A bit shaken on arrival, I decided to let Alyx see me so I could ride back up in the cab. She opened the front door to the condominium, and I slipped in ahead of her, something I'd mastered as a kitten, startling her as expected. She first opened all the shutters and drapes, then started her search upstairs while I started mine downstairs. I went over every inch and then started over. When I looked up, I saw Alyx coming down the stairs and, at the same time, I saw a flash of silver wedged at the base of the first stair step where the carpet met the tile. I had it out by the time Alyx reached the bottom step. The silver object was less than two inches long with a diameter about the size of a pencil. I lifted it up to her and she grabbed it from my teeth. The object safe in her purse, we jumped back in the truck, and she backed out of the driveway. On the way, her phone rang, and when she saw who was calling, she stopped to answer it.

"Alyx, I'd like to see you as soon as possible; I have something I have to tell you in person," I could hear Hunter say through her cell phone.

"All right. I'm on my way back to the store right now."

"I'm leaving the Courthouse now, so I'll meet you there."

Hunter wasn't the type to beg, so I wondered what he had to tell Alyx that he had to tell her face to face? Alyx must have been wondering the same thing and she picked up speed and we were back to the shop in a jiffy.

When Hunter walked into the workroom five minutes after we did, Alyx made room for him on the couch.

"My ex told me that she's been harassing you," he said apologetically.

Alyx looked up, surprised, and turned to face him. "She told you she followed me home and almost sideswiped me?"

Now it was his turn to be surprised. "No, she didn't tell me that. She said she called you several times during the night, but she said nothing about following you. How do you know it was Joann? Did you see the driver?"

"No. It was too dark."

"How about the car? Did you see the color or make?"

Alyx shook her head. "What kind of car does she drive?"

"A black BMW. Alyx ... listen, I'm sorry about all this. I had a long talk with her and she promised not to bother you again. This isn't like Joann; she has more class than that."

"You came here to make excuses for her?"

"No, Alyx, I came here ..."

Alyx put her hand up to stop him from continuing. "She says she's going to stop? What does she want you to do in return?"

He took a deep cleansing breath, "She wants to have dinner with me once or twice a month. I agreed. It seems like precious little if that's what it takes to stop her from bothering you."

Alyx got up slowly, and ponderously walked to her desk as if she were trying to get herself under control.

"*Bothering* me? That's what you call it? I call it *stalking* me. Thanks for trying to protect me, David, but don't do me any favors, I think I'm capable of taking care of myself. Now, if you don't mind I have some work to do."

He didn't move. "It won't last long, Alyx. I promise. She'll get tired of me."

"David, please go."

He lingered at the door. "I'll call you."

"I don't think you should do that for a while."

She turned her back to him, waited for him to leave before she answered the phone, and for the next half hour listened without really hearing a client describe the decorating elements of the private home she was staying at in Palm Beach.

Maggie returned about an hour later and asked her if she'd found anything important in the condominium. Alyx showed her the silver object I'd found that Alyx had now wrapped in a tissue.

"Murfy dug up something very interesting."

"That's a nitroglycerine pill case, isn't it? Where did he find it?" asked Maggie.

"I saw him digging at the base of the stairs where I'd found Althea's body. He alternately tried to dig it out with his paws and pick it up with his teeth. I'm afraid he probably wiped off any prints, or at least smudged them pretty good."

"It's still a clue, one that would have been overlooked otherwise." said Maggie, examining the case closer, without touching it. "It looks like this was attached to something."

"It's like the one Al Jacobs clips to his belt loop," said Alyx, "It might belong to whoever killed Althea."

"Which means the killer would be someone with a heart condition."

"In other words, someone with a bad heart and a motive—no pun intended," joked Alyx.

"Are you going to turn it over to Detective Smarts?"

"Eventually."

"Won't you get in legal trouble if you don't? You should call David and ask him what to do."

Alyx's emotions flared. "I can't ask David...."

With that, Alyx told her all about David's visit, and Maggie put her arm around her shoulders. "David will work it out with his ex, honey. You'll see."

"I'm not so sure he can," said Alyx. "He said he's doing this...this business of allowing himself to be intimidated into seeing his ex-wife for me, but I can't help but think it's because he hasn't disconnected from her yet. She's manipulating him, Maggie. I can't help wondering what else she'll coerce him into doing next. Don't you see where this is going?"

Maggie tried to calm her down. It was apparent Alyx was in no mood for logical arguments; she was hurt, and, yes, she admitted, she was jealous.

"I want him to be free of his ex-wife, not to get more entangled."

She walked out of the workroom and stopped to listen when she overheard a customer ask Bernice what she found most enjoyable about working at Antiques & Designs.

"That's easy. It's the people who walk through the front door," Bernice answered. "I've watched people come and go through that door and wondered about their lives just by the look on their faces. Couples come in sometimes so in tune with each other that they don't even have to speak, and you say to yourself, 'that's how I want my marriage to be. What can I do to make it like that?' I see single women obviously starting over—not sure that they can make it on their own, going forward anyway, and you have to admire their strength and be inspired to get over any little setback you might be experiencing. Then there are the older couples who look so much alike you think they're genetically related; their hair is cut in the same style, and you know they must use the same hair color."

The customer laughed at that. "You should write a book; you certainly have an endless source of material."

"Maybe one of these days," said Bernice, "when I have more time to play."

A wistful smile whispered over Alyx's lips. Was she wondering what her customers saw when she came into view? Did they see a strong, successful woman, or the one scared to take a chance on love? I wondered that myself.

At home that night, I told my housemates about the day's events. They understood that whoever had dropped that pill case must be frantic to get it back, and that meant vigilance on all of our parts. The plan was as before; Pooky, would be in charge of security at home, while Misty and I had the store.

"Cats are glorious creatures—who must on no accounts be underestimated. Their eyes are fathomless depths of cat-world mysteries."
—Lesley Anne Ivory (from *Glorious Cats: The Paintings of Lesley Anne Ivory*)

CHAPTER TWENTY-FOUR: *Far Away Places Not Far from Home*

Mornings at Antiques & Designs are usually slow, and everyone is relaxed, enjoying their morning coffee. Customers trickle in until lunchtime when it starts to get busy. I monitor what goes on whether there is one customer in the store or twenty.

A young couple walked in that I'd never seen before and Alyx greeted them warmly.

"Hi, Alyx, remember us … Melissa and Sean?"

"Of course, I do. We sat at the same table at the masked ball. I'm so glad you decided to stop in."

Melissa looked over at Sean, "We're ready to start looking to buy. I wanted to see those items you told me about, so that when we look for a place to live, we'll know approximately what size and room configuration to look for."

"That's very smart of you."

Melissa put her arm around Sean's waist, her eyes bright with adoration. "It was Sean's idea."

The first item Alyx wanted to show them was Althea's bed. She never made it to the rear of the store, however, as Melissa spotted the slant-front desk, and

Alyx knew she wasn't going to be interested in looking at anything else.

"Oh…honey, isn't it beautiful!" I've always wanted a desk like this. I love all the little pigeon holes, and the leather top. And look at the inlaid work, Sean."

"It's really not my style, a little too delicate for my taste," he said, and then seeing the disappointment on her face, he quickly added, "It's perfect for you, though. If you like it, let's get it. How much is it?"

"I'm sorry; this desk isn't for sale right now. I promise I'll let you know if I decide to sell it. I have some other pieces from the same estate that you might like though," she said pointing them to the rest of the items from Althea's condominium.

Later on, Bernice was back from lunch in a happier mood than the day called for, and in a singsong voice announced, "I know who's opening shop in the old lamp store, and you'll never guess."

"Well, if I'll never guess, you'd better tell me," teased Alyx.

"You're no fun," said Bernice and proceeded to tell her.

"Did you ever watch that travel show where the host traveled to out-of the-way places rather than the more common tourist places in the world?"

"Yes, the show was on TV a couple of years ago on the PBS station, right?" guessed Maggie. "I was sorry to see it go off the air."

Bernice nodded, "The host of that show is the owner of Far Away Places, the new shop where the old lamp store used to be."

"Really?" mused Maggie. "I wonder why he picked this city to open such a store. You'd think after all his travels, he'd want a more sophisticated place than Beachside."

"His father lives here," explained Bernice. "I had lunch with my parents, and it so happens that they live in the same condominium building as his father. They wanted to see his new store, so we stopped in for a few minutes."

"Did you meet him?" asked Alyx, excited.

"Yes. The handsome and charming Jonathan Steele––and he has excellent taste. He has some very unusual items in the store. You should stop in, Alyx. I'm sure you'll find the perfect item for that housewarming gift you mentioned you needed."

"Good idea," replied Maggie. "Thanks, Bernice. I'll do that, and it'll give me the opportunity to solicit his support to save the Blue Heron Yacht Clubhouse. I think it might interest a world traveler, someone who must have an appreciation for history."

"What's the latest on that, anyway?" asked Maggie.

"Can you imagine the oldest clubhouse on the east coast to operate continuously at its original location since it was built in 1897, and efforts to save it have gone nowhere? The only interested developer suggested relocating it via barge, and as he had trouble renting one, he dropped the idea. The contractor of the new building has made another suggestion. He wants to take apart the building, pack up the planks, and reassemble them in replica form next to some other historic buildings he's rescued. Everyone was hoping to see it moved—but this is the next best thing."

"When do you make the final decision?" asked Alyx.

"At next month's meeting when we find out how much it's going to cost," said Maggie. "Of course, the more money we have pledged prior to the meeting, the easier it will be to get *yes* votes."

Alyx interrupted their discussion to go looking for Bernice who had wandered off, and waited for Bernice to finish up with a customer, then asked her, "Do you feel comfortable being left alone for an hour or so?"

"No problem," Bernice quickly agreed.

"I've decided now is as good a time as any to check out that new store you told me about. If anyone's looking for me, have them call me on my cell, and if they don't have my number, tell them to call me here, later."

"Will do, Alyx, and if you're not back, I'll just assume that you and the handsome Jon Steele have run off somewhere exciting." She grinned, savoring the romantic notion.

"Oh, so now it's Jon, is it? Honestly, Bernice, you're worse than Maggie."

Bernice smiled broadly. "Thank you; I consider that a compliment," she said as she sashayed over to assist the two women who'd just walked in the door.

"The cat is mighty dignified until the dog comes by."
—Southern folk saying

CHAPTER TWENTY-FIVE: *An Exotic and Mysterious Shop*

The building that housed Far Away Places was itself as exotic and mysterious as the name implied. It was also located on Ocean Street, about a mile or so from the center of downtown Beachside. Two high-rise condominiums were going up around the corner; evidence of redevelopment in that section of town.

The windowless building shrouded by tropical vegetation, piqued curiosity as to what might be inside. Alyx pushed on the ornately-carved mahogany door and stepped inside a wide-open space. As usual, I was right behind her.

A rumpled-looking man, obviously at home in his surroundings, approached her, smiling.

"Do you always bring your cat with you when you go shopping?"

"This is Murfy," said Alyx, introducing me, "and yes, he does go with me pretty much wherever I go. I hope that's not a problem."

"I'm Jonathan Steele, the owner of this fine establishment and it's no problem at all. If you have any questions about a particular item, I'll be glad to tell you all I know about it."

She introduced herself and added, "My son is buying his first home, and I'm looking for a special housewarming gift. I don't know exactly what; I'll know it when I see it."

"That's exactly how I selected the items in the store. Take your time; I'm sure you'll find the perfect thing."

He returned to the couple he'd been speaking with earlier, and Alyx continued her quick tour of the array of goods from all over the world. A red Oriental rug caught her attention on the first round, and she doubled back to take a closer look. A few minutes later, Jonathan Steele appeared at her side, ready to assist.

"This rug is exactly what I had in mind."

"You've made a good choice. That's a one-of-a-kind made by hand by two women I had the pleasure of meeting and talking to them about their craft."

"I think I saw your show with that segment before it went off the air."

His eyes lit up. "So you watched my show?"

"Yes, whenever I could. I was sorry to see it go."

"I was too at first, until I realized it all turned out for the best. I collected some of these things you see here throughout the years I did the show." He gestured around the room. "and I'll be doing more traveling to buy other items to replenish the stock."

"You really do have unique items. Your store is what our design business needs. I'm sure Maggie, my business partner, and I will be visiting you often."

She paid for her purchase, and he instructed her to drive around back and he would load it in her vehicle. "I'm afraid this is still a one-man show and will be until the business gets going," he said.

Carpet loaded, Alyx slid behind the wheel and rolled down her window. "It was nice meeting you and best wishes on your new adventure. In case you don't already know, owning a business is an adventure. By the way, if you haven't already, I hope you'll join the Downtown Merchants Association. We meet once a month and next month, the topic of discussion is the Blue Heron Yacht Clubhouse. Are you familiar with what's going on with it?"

"Yes, I am. I've been following the story in the newspaper, and I'm curious to know what will be decided. Can I get back to you on the date?"

"Sure, stop in our store anytime. Antiques & Designs is right across from the marina."

"I will, and thank you for visiting my store, Ms. Hille."

Maggie was all smiles when Alyx returned. She said, "I see you didn't get whisked off to a faraway place."

"You and Bernice are incorrigible."

"Yeah, yeah, I know; we're too romantic."

"And maybe I'm not enough;" said Alyx with a sly smile, "however, this one could change my mind."

I relished the look that passed between Maggie and Bernice; a look that said they weren't sure if Alyx was kidding or not. She was of course, wasn't she?

Bernice asked if Alyx had found something for Ethan.

"I found the perfect rug for his entry hall. You want to see it?"

"Yes," Maggie answered, "After we hear all about Jonathan Steele. Bernice gave me the background. What's he really like in person?"

"He has a casual look about him, curly brown hair, cut on the longish side and cocoa-brown eyes, flecked with gold. He's even better-looking in person than he was on TV, and has an abundance of charm. You were right, Bernice, his store is wonderful." She turned to Maggie, "It's the perfect place to find that one final decorative item for a design."

"I'll be so glad when we can shop for that final item for our current client, Mrs. Snob," said Maggie glumly.

Alyx laughed. "She's really gotten to you too, hasn't she?"

"Yes, and I'm ready for a break," Maggie said, as they walked back to the workroom. "I asked George if he wanted to get away for a few days once this project is wrapped up."

"Any place special?"

"We're thinking about taking his boat to the Keys."

"It sounds wonderful."

"You don't mind, then?"

"Not as long as you're back for Althea's estate sale. Seriously, Maggie, go and enjoy yourself; you deserve it."

"I'll let you know when we're leaving and returning as soon as George tells me."

Alyx headed towards the workroom, hesitated, and turned back. "Maggie, we don't pry into each other's business unless invited, so I won't *ask* you. Nevertheless, I sense that something is going on with you and George; whenever you're ready to talk, I'm ready to listen."

Maggie nodded. "I made some fresh vanilla-flavored coffee. Come and join me for a cup, and you can tell me about your ideas for this place."

Alyx pulled a small notebook from her briefcase and flipped it open while Maggie poured the coffee—the aroma irresistible to even a non-coffee drinking cat. Mugs in hand, each women found a place to sit, moving fabrics and magazines aside.

"Okay, this is what I'm thinking," said Alyx. "We already have everything in the store that a customer needs. It's a warm, friendly environment that we could make even more inviting by adding instrumental background music and maybe set up a refreshment bar with coffee and tea. Does it sound good, so far?"

"As nice as it sounds, I don't see how it gets us back to our roots," replied Maggie.

"Hold on, I'm not finished yet," said Alyx. "I'm thinking of providing our customers a distinctive shopping experience. You've heard Bernice say she'd like to get into decorating, so when a customer comes in with a decorating project in mind, the design staff, the new designer and Bernice, will help the customer choose the right items. Those with projects that need special attention can schedule an in-store appointment or a home visit with you or me. In addition, we can keep a record of their colors, fabrics, and measurements for future decorating projects. You and I can take on projects as we see fit.

Maggie scooted to the edge of her chair, "Yeah, and we could sell artwork from local artists, and it doesn't have to be limited to paintings it could be pottery or other artwork for the home."

"So, you like my ideas?" asked Alyx.

"Alyx, I love your ideas. It's the best of all worlds, isn't it? Let's get started as soon as I get back. I'll be glad to put an ad in the paper and do all the interviews."

"Let's talk to Bernice about it. Of course, we'll have to give her a raise for her new duties. Are you okay with that?"

Maggie hesitated before answering. "I gather you've checked with our accountant to make sure we can handle another employee and a raise?" she asked with a raised eyebrow.

Alyx bit her lower lip, "Well, I sort of didn't get that far. You sounded like you could use some cheering up, so I thought you'd feel better if I told you what I was thinking."

Maggie's disappointment was only evident in her voice.

"Now that you got me all excited…I hope we can do it."

"I'll let you know for sure when you get back from the Keys. There's one more idea I'd like to run by you. Since I have my cats in the store, I think it's only fair that our customers should be allowed to bring their pets shopping, if they want to." She saw the skeptical look on Maggie's face and hastened to add, "People don't usually bring misbehaved pets with them, and they'll be required to be on a leash. What harm can they cause?"

Maggie's eyebrows shot up, "Step outside, and look around you, Alyx. Are you kidding or have you lost your mind?"

"What if we limit it to cats?"

"We can't limit it to cats only; we'll upset customers who have dogs," Maggie argued.

In the end, still not convinced it was a good idea, Maggie agreed to try it, but I could tell she was envisioning cat and dogfights, and broken accessories.

So the new "pets welcome" policy was initiated, and just as Maggie had predicted, mayhem broke out a few days later. I was making my rounds of the store and stumbled into the path of a black Main Coon cat several pounds heavier than I was. The cat was surprised to see me and panicked. The commotion attracted customers who stood around watching the Main Coon jumping, leaping and spinning his human around.

There were other incidents that occurred, but the dog relieving himself on a chair leg was the episode that ended "let's allow customers to shop with their pets experiment." Hooray!

"There is no snooze button on a cat who wants
breakfast"
—Unknown

CHAPTER TWENTY-SIX: A Cat is a Cat

The morning was busy and time passed quickly. Before I knew it, Maggie asked Alyx if she was ready for lunch.

"It's only eleven-thirty, but I didn't have any breakfast, and I'm hungry. Is it too early for you?"

"No, it's fine. I was upstairs moving some furniture around, choosing what to have George repair or recycle. I guess the work made me hungry."

"Good. Here's your purse. Let's go."

Alyx laughed. "You're not joking about being hungry, are you?"

As they walked by the display window, Maggie glanced at Misty sitting tall next to the candelabrum where she'd been all morning, scrutinizing each passerby, with a puzzled look flitting across her face.

"Misty hasn't moved from that spot since I came in this morning," said Maggie. "And Murfy is at the door trying to get his leash off the hook. Cats don't do that; dogs do that."

Alyx shrugged her shoulders. "I don't know what to tell you, Maggie."

I knew what to tell her if I could talk. It's so unfair— dogs aren't the only intelligent house pets. Some cats are just as clever; we just don't let on that we are, thereby, we get away with doing more things we shouldn't. My efforts paid off, and Alyx grabbed my leash and off we went.

The Beachside Café was busy as usual. The restaurant had a pleasant ambiance with exposed brick walls and a planked wood floor. The counter was a rich, dark mahogany with a brass foot railing. A booth opened up and Alyx said, "It's so busy in here; maybe it's better if we get something to go. I don't feel comfortable sitting down for lunch with Murfy. There are a lot of tourists in town, and we're getting some funny looks."

They ordered their favorite and mine—shrimp salad on cheddar bread. Novie, the owner of the Café, brought the food out when it was ready.

"Isn't it nice to see all these tourists back in town?"

"I know what you mean," said Alyx. "After that last hurricane, everybody wondered if we'd ever see tourists again, and that one didn't even hit us. It seems to me that it doesn't really matter where they make landfall, we're affected by any hurricane that even comes close to Florida."

Alyx said, "That's because those monsters are big enough to cover the whole state!" She added, "I wonder how many insurance policies will be cancelled, next time."

"Our condo insurance more than doubled last year and so did the insurance I carry for the inside of my unit, although it won't cost twice as much to replace the contents," said Maggie.

A man waiting for his take-out order, someone I didn't know, joined the conversation.

"The insurance companies have changed their philosophy of doing business. It used to be they bet against something happening while we bet it would happen. Now it's the reverse; they bet that something will happen and charge accordingly. They have us right where they want us and they know it. People are too scared not to carry insurance, and rightly so."

Maggie redirected the conversation to Novie. "Speaking of insurance, have you heard anything more about the diamond robbery?"

"Chet Hall came in for lunch yesterday, and I asked him about it. He said the police haven't caught the thief, and they have no leads—they think he had a driver waiting for him outside, or he disappeared into one of the crowded businesses next to the jewelry store. They came in here and asked all of us if we'd seen anyone fitting the description they gave us—we didn't."

"The police talked to all of us as well," said Maggie, "and at our next meeting, Alyx and I are going to suggest that the Merchants Association make a formal request for a greater police presence, especially during peak tourist periods."

Novie said that after what had happened, she didn't think there would be any opposition to the suggestion.

Later after lunch and back at the shop, Maggie's tone of voice said it all when she told Alyx, "She doesn't like the tiles in the courtyard."

An audible groan escaped Alyx, "Too bad. We had nothing to do with that. She picked out her own contractor to do that job. I knew we shouldn't have let her do that." Alyx looked around the room, and her eyes fell on the rich-toned fabric left over from another job. "Not to worry, Maggie, I have the solution. We simply recover all the cushions with that striped, brick red fabric left over from the Carabba's home."

"Do we have enough?"

"Just enough. Do you want to show the fabric to our client first?"

"Not today."

"Alyx, you're a genius, you know."

"No, just a good designer, and so are you."

"Do you sometimes think we're too good?"

"You mean because we're so busy?"

Maggie nodded, "Alyx I need a break after this job."

"I know you do. It's hard dealing with the varied personalities of the customers on a daily basis. There are some I'd like to ban permanently from entering the store."

"That overweight, screaming man who insisted on buying Althea's desk, for example?"

"Exactly."

"Listen, I have a few things to take care of, and I think I'll do that now if you don't mind," said Maggie.

"Okay, Maggie, I'll see you later."

Alyx measured the fabric, put it back on the shelf, and then pulled the tissue-wrapped pillbox from her purse; she set it down in front of her and perched on the edge of the chair behind the desk. She folded her arms on the desk, and I placed my paw on her forearm, both of us staring at the silver object.

"What do you know, fur-baby? Did you sense something else when you found this?"

Alyx abruptly stood, knocking me off balance, and the flash of insight that was starting to form in my brain disappeared as quickly as it had appeared.

Maggie came back to the store a bit later, to pick up some information she'd forgotten, making small talk while she looked for it.

"I had a heartwarming experience at lunch yesterday," she told Alyx. "I meant to tell you earlier but forgot."

"Where did you go?"

"I had an errand to run for George, and on the way I stopped at a beach side diner called Betty's. The first thing I noticed when I walked in was the clientele—they were all senior citizens."

Alyx raised an eyebrow at that.

"I know that's not an unusual sight around here. What was unusual was that all the servers looked to be in their seventies, and the cashier had to be well over eighty.

"So what happened?"

"Nothing happened. The interaction among the servers and with the cook was touching. In fact, I thought they were all related, so when I left I had to ask, and it turns out that Betty, the cashier, was the original owner of the diner back in the sixties when they were located on Main Street. She sold the place ten years later, and the new owners moved the diner to its current location. What I find amazing is that all the employees that worked for Betty at the Main Street location stayed on to work for the new owners. No one left, Alyx. They are all still there."

"That's a nice story. It says a lot about Betty and the new owners, doesn't it?"

"We're nice employers. Do you think Nelda and Bernice will be that loyal?"

"Work ethics aren't what they used to be. Let's just say, I won't take it personally if they decide to leave."

Maggie eventually found what she was looking for and left. Alyx went looking for Bernice and waited for her to finish up with a customer, then asked, "Do you feel comfortable being left alone for an hour or so?"

"No problem."

"I have to run a few errands. If anyone's looking for me, have them call me on my cell, and if they don't have the number, tell them to call me here, later."

*"Cats are a mysterious kind of folk. There is more
passing in their minds that we are aware of."*
—Walter Scott

CHAPTER TWENTY-SEVEN: *An Amateur Sleuth
with a Cat for a Partner*

Alyx turned over the small, silver pill case to
Detective Smarts—not mentioning that I was the one
who'd found it.

"Do you think the killer might have left it behind?"
she asked.

"Not necessarily; it could have been dropped by
anyone at any time."

"So, it doesn't help anything?"

"I didn't say that, Ms. Hille. Many other things have
to come together, such as a suspect, a possible motive,
and an opportunity. Of course, we'll check it for
prints."

"It seems to me, Detective Smarts, you're taking a
lot of time to put those things together, unlike your
action in my son's case."

Detective Smarts expelled a breath of air from his
puffed cheeks. He leaned forward in his chair and
looked her directly in the eyes. "Ms. Hille, I'm truly
sorry about what happened to your son. At the time, he
was the only suspect with motive and opportunity. If it
were to happen again, I'd have to say I'd do the same
thing. As far as my reluctance to talk to you about the
case—I see you as an amateur sleuth with a cat for a

partner. No excuses, I just can't take either one of you seriously."

Alyx stared at him for a full five seconds before she shook her head and laughed. "I guess I can't blame you when you put it that way."

She stood, slipped her bag over her shoulder, and at the same time, extended her hand. "If I can help in any way, as a concerned citizen, let me know. As far as my cat is concerned, I can't make any promises; he has a mind of his own."

The handshake said they had a temporary truce. As for me, I didn't care what Detective Smarts thought of my detective skills. I had a job to do, and I intended to do it.

Unlike Smarts, there were several suspects with motive and opportunity on my list. All I needed was a little help to ferret them out into the open. Although I'd figured out that Simon wasn't as altruistic as he wanted me to believe, it was necessary that I spend more time with him and his friends see what I could learn. I fervently hoped that I was strong enough to resist the temptation to join forces with him.

Later that night, I was so preoccupied with my own thoughts on the way to the shed, that I wasn't aware I was being followed, until I saw Pooky and Misty situate themselves outside the shed so they could hear but not be seen. Misty had questioned me during the day and must have figured out that I was meeting with Simon and his friends. She probably thought I'd lied to her and I was still planning to join him.

Awed and confused, the girls were silent throughout the whole process. I had no way to warn them that they were being shadowed—my worst fear was realized when they filed into the dilapidated shack. Six huge Siamese cats sat in statuesque poses, their blue, laser-like eyes aimed at their captives, prohibiting any movement;

Wide-eyed with fear, my housemates held their heads high. I made a quick assessment of the situation and decided on a course of action. Before Simon could say anything, I pounced in front of the felines and in a loud roar that whipped their ears back, demanded to know why they'd followed me.

Misty stepped forward and hissed that she wanted to know if I was going to join Simon, and Pooky insisted that it wasn't totally Misty's idea. Then they looked at each other disheartened, unaware of my motives, when I said that I didn't believe them. Simon grinned when I told him I wanted to take them home and teach them a lesson or two about privacy. I promised Simon it wouldn't happen again and no one stood in our way as I led them both out. Once clear of the shed, the girls were off in a blur. I was proud of them. They were obviously scared, but not intimidated.

I was in no hurry. The felines were well ahead of me—which was fine—because I needed the time to clear my mind. Maybe I should have told them everything. I should have known that Misty wouldn't let it go, but never did I believe that anything could have motivated Pooky to leave the house. The most important lesson I'd learned that night is that true friendship—human and otherwise—is a gift to cherish.

The trip home was uneventful; no animal or human challenged our right to the night. I arrived home a few minutes behind the other two and found them waiting on the lanai. There was no arguing when I flatly stated that I would discuss everything with them in the morning. I slid the latch on the pet door closed, with no human any wiser to our recent outdoor excursion.

The following morning while Alyx was busy doing other things, I reassured Misty that I hadn't lied to her; I told her I had to make Simon think that I was still considering leaving so that I could learn more from him about Althea. She said she trusted me, but she had no idea what Simon was teaching me, and as far as Althea's murder case went, she wanted to help and to let her know what I needed her to do. Then she bounced away, her string trailing behind her, the same-old Misty, yet so different.

At the shop, Alyx and Maggie were busy rearranging a few items on the floor, and Maggie was trying to keep things positive as they pushed and shoved furniture around. When Alyx complained about the work, Maggie said moving furniture was not her favorite thing to do either, yet undoubtedly it was worth the effort if the item sold. Nevertheless, they were delighted to see Mary Zenn walk in, a big smile on her face.

"You look like you won the lottery. What's up?"

"It's even better than winning the lottery," answered Mary, plopping down on the couch they'd just pushed to a new location, the grin she walked in with not leaving her face.

"Maggie, let's finish this later."

"No problem; I'll take good news over moving furniture any day."

"Okay, are you ready for this?" asked Mary.

"Yes," they answered in unison.

"Do you remember the paintings you sold to the man from Palm Beach?"

"Yes, Maggie said he asked for your card. Does he want to buy more of your work?" asked Alyx.

"Oh, it's much better than that. John Rictus is the owner of the Rictus Art Gallery and he wants my artwork to be part of his next exhibition!"

"Mary, that's wonderful!"

Alyx hugged her. Maggie congratulated her and waited to hear more.

"The show is in three months, and he wants me to do as many new paintings as I can until then. Apparently, they get more artsy tourists than we get here in Beachside," she said glancing at the unsold paintings on the wall.

"I'll send invitations, and I hope you both can come."

Mary cleared her throat, "Do you think you guys can help me with my hair and clothes on the night of my show?"

"Sure, we can. Maggie is the fashion plate around here. I'll be glad to go with you to my stylist Enzo; he's great at makeovers. He'll give you what you want done in his special way," she laughed. "I'll make an appointment for the week before, so you have time to adjust to your cut."

The look on Mary's face said she'd assumed too much. "You don't want your hair cut, do you?"

Mary hung her head a little, "I thought just taming it a little would help. I'm an artist. Artists are supposed to look weird." As she said that, her head came up, "Thanks, Alyx, I think I'll go as myself," and then she added, "Maybe you and Maggie can help me look like me, only better."

Maggie and Alyx exchanged looks, and Maggie nodded. "Speaking for Maggie and me, it's a deal," said Alyx.

"A cat can maintain a position of curled up somnolence on your knee until you are nearly upright. To the last minute she hopes your conscience will get the better of you and you will settle down again."
—Pam Brown

CHAPTER TWENTY-EIGHT: *David Hunter's Competition*

Jonathan Steele walked in, coincidently dressed like Alyx. His khakis and tee shirt matched Alyx's outfit, except her khakis were cropped, and her shirt was tucked in. Misty ran towards him to sniff his shoes, his pants and then his hands as the man reached down to stroke her head.

"Welcome to *my* fine establishment," Alyx said, smiling and swinging her arm wide.

"Very nice," he nodded appreciatively.

"Feel free to browse, if you want."

"Today is not a good day to look around as I only have an hour for lunch. I think I mentioned that I don't have any help at the store, so I can't leave whenever I want. I do close for an hour everyday at this time; I'll definitely look around next time though. I know it's too late for lunch, but how about a cup of coffee next door. I hear their homemade muffins are the best in town," said Jonathan. "I'm interested in hearing what you have to say about the next Association meeting."

Alyx didn't hesitate to accept the invitation for coffee. She reached for a copy of the meeting agenda from the stack on the counter and handed it to him. He folded it and put it in his pocket.

"I'll be ready to go in a minute, I have to tell Nelda I'm leaving and put Murfy on a leash."

They walked out smiling with me bouncing along beside them. Alyx was explaining about my protectiveness, and I don't think she saw David Hunter get out of his car across the street—but he saw her. He stood there for a moment, and then got back in the car and drove off.

"I'm glad you could get away. Do you always have two people in the store?" asked Steele.

"As often as we can manage it without making it a hardship for anyone. Our design business keeps Maggie and me out of the store more than we like. We have two wonderful, trustworthy employees and we're possibly looking to hire a third to help with the decorating part. Maggie and I both miss the hunt for antiques and collectibles and we want to do more of that."

"That's the same with me, except I search for items that will someday become an antique or collectible. I still intend to travel; I'm limiting my trips to faraway places in this country for the time being though."

"Given the state of the world these days, I'd say that's a wise decision on your part."

They talked about the business climate on Ocean Street, but most of the conversation was about his travels. Alyx asked him about the Taj Mahal.

"Stop me if I start to sound like a tour guide."

Alyx laughed; she was doing a lot of that.

"As you know, the Taj Mahal is a mausoleum."

She said she didn't, and he continued. "The Mughal emperor Shah Jahan had it built in memory of his wife, who died giving birth to their fourteenth child. It took twenty thousand men and seventeen years to build it. The main building material is white marble inlaid with red sandstone, jasper, jade, crystal, turquoise, sapphires, and diamonds. In all, twenty-eight kinds of rare, semi-precious and precious stones were used."

"Do they allow people to tour the inside?"

"Yes, they do. There's a central chamber, a crypt immediately below and four octagonal corner rooms originally intended to house the graves of other royal family members. In the center are the cenotaphs of Shah Jahan and his wife, Mumtaz Mahal. According to custom, she rests immediately below the dome and he is to the left and a little higher. Above the tombs is a Cairene lamp, which is not supposed to burn out. Both tombs are exquisitely inlaid with semiprecious stones, and surrounded by a marble screen of trellis work."

He leaned back in his seat, "I hope I haven't told you more than what you wanted to hear," he said apologetically as one who loves his subject matter, not sure when to stop.

"No, not at all. I've never known anyone who's actually seen it. Is it true that the emperor planned on building a black marble Taj for himself?"

He shrugged, "It's often mentioned in historical guidebooks, but many scholars believe it's a myth. What do you think?"

"I think that he built the mausoleum in memory of his beloved wife and is happy to be buried with her."

"I agree."

Maggie was standing behind the cash register grinning at Alyx like the proverbial Cheshire cat when we returned. "Nelda said you were having coffee with a very good-looking man who wasn't David," she said.

Two creases formed between her eyes at the mention of David's name, and then disappeared as she told Maggie about Jonathan Steele.

"He's so interesting… and the more he talked, the more I liked him. I started noticing little things about him, like the way his eyes crinkled at the corners when he smiled. I noticed he used his hands a lot—strong, with well-manicured fingernails. I had to fight the urge to touch the dimple on his chin to the point that I had to fold my hands on my lap for fear of actually doing it."

She suddenly stopped talking as if she'd said more than she wanted to say.

"That's enough about Jonathan Steel. What's up with you?"

"I just spoke with George, and we'll be leaving for the Keys this Friday—back in a few days. I asked Nelda if she could help you with Althea's estate sale Saturday, and she said she would. Now, are you sure you're okay with this?"

"Yes, don't worry. Go have fun. And don't forget; I'm here when you're ready to talk."

Maggie hugged her. "I'm hopeful that it will be resolved by the time we get back."

*" 'What's your name?' Coraline asked the cat. 'Look,
I'm Coraline. Okay? 'Cats don't have names,' it said.
'No?' said Coraline. 'No,' said the cat. 'Now you
people have names. That's because you don't know who
you are. We know who we are, so we don't need
names.'"*
—Neil Gaiman, *Coraline*

CHAPTER TWENTY-NINE: *Murfy's List of Suspects*

Althea's next-door neighbor, Bill, was talking to a
woman with tomato red hair, wearing a pink sleeveless
housedress, the hot pink nail polish a perfect match to
her lips. We drove up in front of Althea's
condominium.

"Hi, Bill," said Alyx. "How are you doing?"

"Fine. Fine. At my age, what else can I say that
won't bore you to death?"

Alyx introduced herself to the red haired woman.

"Wanda, here, was telling me about Althea's niece,"
Bill said.

"What about Althea's niece?" asked Alyx.

He looked at Wanda for an answer. "She and a
young man were here earlier today," she answered in a
gravelly smoker's voice.

"She must have decided she wanted something
before the estate sale," suggested Alyx.

"If she did, she didn't take it with her. It looked to
me like they were angry about something," said Wanda.

"They came out, slamming the front door shut, and then slamming their car doors."

"Did they say anything?"

"I heard her son say something about it not being his fault."

"How did you know it was Carole's son?"

"I happened to be outside when they came over one day," explained Wanda, "and when they left, Althea told me who they were, and she didn't seem too happy about the visit, either. The young man—Carole's son—was here with another man the night before her body was found."

"What did the other man look like?" asked Alyx.

"I was walking my dog, and not paying attention. All I noticed about him was that he was rather portly."

"Did the police talk to you?"

"Yes, and I told them all this."

Alyx chatted with Bill and Wanda for a few more minutes before we went inside.

"Okay, fur-baby," she said to me, "let's see what else you can find today."

She stood in the living room thinking aloud. "What were they looking for—do you think it was that pill case— or something else?"

I raced up the stairs and she followed slowly talking to herself.

"Okay, let's think about this. As things stand, Carole will inherit quite a sum of money, and due to her family's financial problems, she had motive to kill Althea. For the same reason, Carole's son could have killed her so his mother could get access to the money; that pill case could belong to either one of them, and they came back looking for it."

I agreed with her assessment. It was also possible that Althea's long-lost son had gotten in touch with Carole—she would be, after all, his cousin and only family. Maybe Carole was worried that Althea's son would contest the will, and so she came back looking for something having to do with that.

Carole and her son weren't the only suspects on my list. There was also Carole's husband—his own financial situation could be worse than Carole knew or admitted to. He could have killed Althea.

Finally, although I had nothing concrete to go on yet, there was one other person who had motive and opportunity—Althea's son. According to the letter from the private investigation firm, he'd planned to see Althea. He could be the murderer—his motive the same as the others—money.

Alyx had her question answered as to what Carole and her son were looking for as soon as she entered Althea's room and saw the contents of the lingerie chest she'd previously boxed, spilled on the bed.

"They most definitely were looking for something, weren't they, Murfy?"

I meowed in agreement. No sense in looking through that; it looked like they did a good job. Regardless, she quickly went through it as she put it all back into the box, not bothering to sort it this time, and found nothing to back-up the scenarios she'd mentioned—or mine—for that matter.

"Well, that's that. The only thing left to do is to go to Carole's house and find out if either her son or husband has a heart problem."

Alyx paused in the living room, and her eyes fell on a small Imari porcelain bowl sitting on a console table against the stairwell. The bowl didn't have a tag, and she picked it up for closer inspection. When she did, an amber bead fell out.

I figured the bead had broken off of something, and when I saw a basket of jewelry sitting on the coffee table, I called attention to it with my 'I want something' meow that I'd trained her to recognize.

She rifled through it, didn't find anything to match the amber bead, and dropped it in the basket. Something must have popped in her mind as she did that. She shook her head as if to clear it, and said, "Come on, Murfy, let's get out of here," expecting me to follow. I wasn't ready to go yet though, and I turned my back, and quickly pawed through the jewelry until I found the bead that Alyx had tossed in the basket. I secreted it in my mouth thinking it would serve as evidence later, if needed.

"The dog has a human master; the cat is the master of his human."
—Murfy

CHAPTER THIRTY: *Antiques & Designs–A Midnight Visit*

Alyx sat up in bed, none of us sure what she'd heard until the doorbell rang again. She grabbed her robe and peered out the kitchen window before going to the door or turning on any lights. A Beachside police cruiser was in her driveway and she hurried to the front door.

The shorter of the two officers spoke first," Are you Alyx Hille?"

"Yes. What's wrong? Did something happen to my son, Ethan?"

The officer introduced himself and his partner.

"No, ma'am, we're here to report a break-in at your store on Ocean Street."

She took a deep breath, "Okay, tell me what happened," she said, opening the door wider, inviting them into the foyer.

"We were patrolling the area and didn't see anything outstanding until we drove around to the parking area in the rear of the stores and saw the back door to your establishment wide open. We investigated and found no one inside. We believe the perpetrator or perpetrators fled when they saw us. We'd like you to come with us and identify any missing items for our report."

She wished Maggie were around. As if he read her mind, the taller officer said, "We also tried to contact Maggie Broeck; there was no answer."

"Maggie is my business partner and she's out of town, but you already know that, don't you?"

They gave her one of those polite smiles that isn't a real smile and fools no one.

She started to walk away and remembered her manners. "Excuse me while I put some clothes on. I'll meet you there."

"A cat sees no good reason why it should obey another animal, even if it does stand on two legs."
—Sarah Thompson

CHAPTER THIRTY-ONE: *The Estate Sale*

Early Saturday, the morning of the estate sale, Alyx called Maggie to tell her about the break-in.

"I'll have Bernice take inventory today to make sure nothing is missing," she said. "The items from Althea's condominium are in shambles, though. The furniture was turned over on its side, drawers pulled out, chair seats removed, apparently ready to be torn apart, possibly interrupted by the appearance of the patrol car..." She paused. "They searched under, behind and in all the drawers."

"I'm speechless," replied Maggie. "What could they have wanted?"

"I think someone was looking for something that belonged to Althea."

"So you don't think it was a robbery?"

Alyx took a deep breath before answering. "No, I don't. At first, I thought it might have been bored teenagers out for an evening of mischief, but now I think maybe not. The police are calling it a break-in, and said they'll conduct an investigation accordingly. They did say they found the alarm disabled. Apparently, it's an old-fashioned model, and anyone could have disabled it. I don't necessarily agree with that; I couldn't."

"I'm sorry, Alyx. I shouldn't have left you with the estate sale going on—and now this to deal with too. We'll leave right away, and I'll investigate the cost of putting in a new alarm system as soon as I get back."

"No, it's not necessary for you to leave, Maggie. I can handle it. The only reason I called was to let you know about it. If I need you, I promise I'll call. I'll let you know if there are any developments and don't worry, okay?"

Although Alyx rushed to get to Althea's place early, Nelda was already at her condominium when we arrived for the estate sale.

"I've got coffee and pumpkin muffins," Alyx announced, and handed Nelda the bag of muffins.

They unloaded and set up a card table in the garage, grabbed a couple of chairs from the kitchen, and Alyx tied my leash to her chair, which was totally unnecessary since I wasn't about to go anywhere with a crowd of people stomping around, not watching where they stepped, I'm sure.

The women barely had time to take a sip of coffee when a caravan of trucks and vans arrived.

"Fasten your seatbelt, Nelda. Here we go."

Nelda took a bite of the pumpkin muffin and smiled. "Got coffee. Got food. I'm ready."

Most of the early birds were local dealers hunting for bargains. Alyx said she remembered all those times when she'd arrive at a sale at the advertised time, and half the items would have been gone because the dealers beat her to the sale and made tempting offers that the homeowners couldn't refuse.

She ignored the slamming car doors and the murmuring of the mini-crowd until one man—the owner of the collectibles store down the street from

Antiques & Designs—asked in a loud, brusque manner, why she wasn't letting them in.

"In the interest of those who want to buy items for their own use and not for resale, I've decided to make it fair, and open the sale at the time stated in the ads. According to my watch, it's not nine o'clock yet."

"Aw, come on. You know how it works; this isn't the only sale going on."

"It's the one I'm running, and I'm opening at the time advertised."

The man clenched his fists, pushed past a couple of other people, made a show of slamming his truck door, and peeled away. No one said anything, except the thumbs-up sign from the young mother in the back of the group.

As the day progressed, the estate sale was going well. Most everything sold for the asking price, and by the middle of the day when the crowd had trickled down to one or two people at a time, Alyx started marking items half-price to move them more quickly.

Alyx and Nelda had everything wrapped up by three in the afternoon. Nelda was helping her carry a few items to her truck, when she saw a note under the windshield wipers and handed it to Alyx, who scanned it and shoved it in her pocket without comment.

"Thanks again for helping out, Nelda. I hope it wasn't too much for you. Estate sale customers can be trying." She turned, unlocked the car door, buckled my carrier into the passenger seat, and climbed in without further conversation. She didn't notice that Nelda hadn't left, and rested her forehead on the steering wheel.

"Did that rude man from this morning leave you a nasty note?" said Nelda through the window.

"Don't worry, Nelda; it's not the first time I've made someone angry. Thank you for all your help. You worked hard today. Enjoy what's left of the day, and I'll see you Monday."

Alyx drove straight to the police station, and she asked to see Detective Smarts. He wasn't in, so she left a message for him to call her as soon as possible regarding a threatening note someone had left her.

"Meow is like aloha—it can mean anything."
—Hank Ketchum

CHAPTER THIRTY-TWO: *A Welcome Diversion*

Alyx looked tired and for good reason. First, someone had broken into the store, and now a threatening note had been left on her truck. Clearly fascinated by Jonathan Steele, she hadn't hesitated to accept his dinner invitation, but now she seemed to be having second thoughts, as I watched her move slowly around her bedroom. She pulled an outfit out of the closet and then put it back, she dialed a number and then disconnected it before it rang. In the end, she stepped into the shower. Coming out with a thick cotton towel wrapped around her, she applied color to her eyes and lips.

The female cats were no longer interested in her wardrobe, now that she'd purged her closet of all the unattractive clothes. In keeping with her more casual style, her wardrobe was now up-to-date and flattering.

The doorbell chimed and we all followed her to the door, Pooky anxious to meet the new man and ready to dislike him. As it turned out, Steele came with a bag of treats in his pocket and the two of them left for the Ethiopian restaurant having made three new friends.

As a precaution, I had asked Gemma, one of Pooky's outdoor cat friends, to keep an eye on Alyx when she was away from me if she could.

Gemma had ingratiated herself with Hunter's assistant, Dorinda, when I gave her a job to do that involved surveillance of the lawyer's office. She visited Pooky on occasion, and I was glad to hear that now she had a home when she wanted one, and could depend on regular meals—no cat should have to scrounge for food.

When they returned from their date, Alyx invited Jonathan in for coffee. They engaged in small talk while she prepared the coffee and it was ready within minutes. She watched him stir three teaspoons of sugar into his cup and asked him what motivated him to start traveling.

"I was born in Africa. While in college, and against my parent's wishes—I might add—I decided to visit my birthplace. I loved the experience and knew that it was what I wanted to do for the rest of my life. So when I graduated, I got a job with an import-export company in Chicago, and the rest is history, as they say."

"Did you tell me that Lithuania was the last country you visited?"

"Yes, that's right. I was there about a month ago. I met some wonderful artists whom I hope I can continue to do business with." He shifted in his chair, moving a little closer. "That's enough about me; now tell me about you. Are you a transplant like most of us here in Florida?"

"There's really not much to tell. I was born and raised in Lansing, Michigan. My brother, Tom, and his family were already living in this area when I moved here. My ex and I had often talked about moving to a warmer climate and since our son was five and starting school, we thought it an appropriate time to make our move. Five years later, I found myself a single mom, on my own. I went back to school to become a designer and met Maggie. We both already had a large collection of things and talked about someday owning our own business. One day, I was walking along Ocean Street and saw a building for sale, made an offer, and as you said, the rest is history."

They both reached for their coffee. Alyx put her cup down. "I know you're not married now; have you ever been?" she asked.

He shook his head. "There have been significant others. I'm not seeing anyone now. How about you? I assume, since you're here with me, there's no one special in your life?"

She lowered her eyes before she answered. "No, there isn't."

The rest of the evening was devoted to general conversation—business, the area, and other light subjects.

Alyx tried to stifle a yawn and lost. She apologized and explained why she was so tired.

"Do you often conduct estate sales?"

"No, actually, we don't. This was a special case; Althea was a friend."

He blinked in quick succession. Alyx didn't appear to have seen his reaction, probably due to her tiredness, but I did.

"Did the estate sale include all the contents of the house?"

"No. The better pieces we bought outright and are in our store—all together in one spot."

"Did you find a favorite piece?"

She smiled, "Yes, the bed," and she went on to describe it.

She yawned again, this time openly and no excuses.

"Okay, Alyx, I'd better go before you fall asleep on me. That wouldn't be good for my ego," he said, trying to sound hurt.

"Somehow, I don't think that's a problem for you."

She walked him to the door, and he took her hand in both of his, "I've enjoyed your company. Maybe we can do it again, soon?"

"I'd like that."

She locked the door, turned off the lights and went straight to bed.

"There's no need for a piece of sculpture in a home that has a cat."
—Wesley Bates

CHAPTER THIRTY-THREE: *The Problem That Wasn't a Problem*

Alyx was on the phone when I ventured into the workroom the next day.

"Maggie, where are you calling from? Is everything all right?"

"I'm home and I'm fine," Maggie said.

"Home? What happened, sweetie? I told you I was taking care of everything. I hope you didn't come home just because of what happened."

"No, that's not why I'm back," I heard Maggie say from the receiver. "Do you have time to talk? I'll bring lunch."

"I'll make the time."

Maggie lived in a one-bedroom condominium on the ocean. Her attractive seventh-floor condominium, decorated in a sleek modern style was second only to the ocean view from the floor-to-ceiling sliding glass doors across the width of the living room. Traffic was usually heavy around lunchtime, and the ten-minute trip took us twenty minutes plus the time it took to pick up the lunch order at the Cuban Sandwich Shop.

After greeting each other with hugs, Alyx didn't waste any time getting to the point.

"Okay, what's wrong?"

"George's son, Erik, is thinking about enrolling in college here in Florida and asked if he could stay with him for a year or two, so he can save money to pay for the next two years of school, and George told him that he can stay for as long as he wants."

"I don't understand. Why are you so upset about that? Granted, you won't have the same privacy you have now, but you can work it out, can't you?" Alyx took a sip of lemonade and set it down.

Maggie did the same, except she held on to hers and paced to the door and back.

"That's not it. It's that I don't know how to behave around a nineteen-year-old. I've never had any kids, and I don't really know him; I've only spent a few days with him. I don't know how to be a mother; I don't even know how to cook. What if he hates me?"

"Maggie, he's not going to hate you. To begin with, you don't have to mother him; he has a mother already, and, secondly, George loves you. Did he say anything that sounded like he's changing his mind?"

She shook her head, drained her plastic cup, and dropped it in the wastebasket. "He has no idea why I wanted to come home. Since I'm the one who suggested going in the first place, he had no problem with me changing my mind." She smiled. "Sometimes I think he's too good to be true."

"The old Maggie would have said he was 'too good for *her*,' and that's why I can say I think you're experiencing commitment jitters."

"I should have stayed here and helped you instead of running away."

Alyx waved away the sentiment and suggested they eat lunch. Maggie took a bite of the crunchy lunchmeat sandwich and asked if there was any new information about the break-in or the estate sale.

"The sale went fine. Nelda did a great job. Almost everything sold for the price marked." Then, she hesitated, "Something odd did happen though." She pulled the note from her purse and handed it to Maggie to read.

Maggie read the short note out loud: "SHE'S GONE AND SO ARE HER THINGS—LEAVE IT ALONE OR ELSE ... Oh, my! Alyx! You did tell Detective Smarts about this, right?"

"Well, I tried. I left him a message but I haven't heard back from him yet."

She picked up her cell phone and handed it to her. "Call him again, Alyx."

"All right, Maggie, I'll give him a call if you promise to call George and talk to him about the changes you'll have to make with his son coming—and be sure to tell him you'll be joining him more often on his picking jaunts."

Alyx made the call, and this time her message said it was urgent.

"Honest as the cat when the meat's out of reach."
—Old English Saying

CHAPTER THIRTY-FOUR: *A Gift From a Far Away Place*

The store closed at six on Sundays, and Alyx usually had dinner with Ethan and, most times, his girlfriend, Nicki. About once a month, she and Ethan got together with her brother, Tom, and his wife Susan. I knew she was glad for any time she had with Ethan—truth was, she missed his company. At the same time, she was happy to see him settling down, looking forward to spoiling her future grandchildren in a way she hadn't been able to spoil Ethan due to her financial situation while he was growing up.

Ethan called earlier in the day, and told her not to cook anything, since he couldn't stay for dinner. When he arrived, the girls and I greeted him as usual at the door, looking for the treat he always brought when he visited, and he didn't disappoint.

Ethan asked Alyx about the estate sale, and then asked about her date with Jonathan.

"Jonathan is an interesting man. He's been to countries I've only heard about, and some I haven't."

"What about David? Are you still to seeing him?"

Alyx had never liked discussing the romantic part of her life with her son, and rarely did. She quickly changed the subject by telling him about the Ethiopian restaurant they'd been to, how they served the food all on one large platter with no utensils, with only pancake-like bread, folded like a napkin, which was used as a tool to grab the food.

"I expected the restaurant to be along the same showy lines as what you'd find at a tourist attraction—but it wasn't. It's small, inconspicuous and tucked away in an out-of-the-way kind of neighborhood about an hour's drive from here. You and Nicki should go try it."

Mom, you know she doesn't like anything except basic food. The most exotic thing she'll eat is spaghetti."

"That's not exotic; that's American."

He laughed. "Exactly."

He asked her if there was anything new on Althea's case, and she told him everything she knew about it and who she suspected—omitting, I noticed, the part about the note.

Later, Alyx made a sandwich and heated a can of tomato soup while I did some thinking about what Ethan had said earlier regarding Jonathan Steele. We evidently both thought it an odd coincidence that she could meet two people in Beachside who had both lived in the same city on another continent. She took the last bite of her chicken salad sandwich, just as the doorbell sounded its Westminster chime.

Jonathan Steele stood at the door with a grin, a bag of *Lilly* espresso coffee and a box of *Amaretti* cookies.

"Italy was one of the last places I visited," he said, offering her the coffee and cookies.

"Well, thank you," she said, hesitating a moment, not sure what to do. "Would you like to come in and have some coffee and cookies?"

"I'd love to. It's been a long day—a very busy day."

She prepared the coffee, put a few cookies on a plate, and carried them to the living room along with the espresso.

He took a sip from the demitasse cup, "It's very gracious of you to invite me in without my calling you first. I took a chance, and I'm glad you didn't disappoint me."

"Well, I am sort of surprised. Earlier, I was telling my son about you and your store, and he mentioned the fact that you're the second person I've met here in Beachside with a direct connection to Africa."

I watched his face closely when she said that.

"Africa is a big nation."

"Strange enough, my friend lived in Sierra Leone, where you said you were born."

"What's your friend's name?" he asked, showing only polite curiosity.

"Her name is—was—Althea Burns. She died a few days before Christmas."

"I'm sorry to hear that. Was she a close friend of yours?"

The way he said that made me think that it was the right time to give Alyx the amber bead that we'd found in Althea's condominium. I ran to the laundry room where I'd stored it for safekeeping. I realized I couldn't drop it at her feet in front of Jonathan—I had to get her to the laundry room alone. So, I did my loud, frantic meowing routine, but unfortunately, only Misty and Pooky showed up. I told them what was going on, and soon there were three cats frantically meowing. Alyx still didn't come right away, but eventually she did and she looked annoyed when she did. I pointed out the amber bead. I was glad to see her pocket the bead when Jonathan called out and asked if everything was all right. I was sure she got my message when she whispered, "Good job, kitty-cats."

The three of us ran ahead to the living room where Jonathan remained seated.

"I remember hearing you say that the last place you visited was Lithuania. What are they best known for exporting?" asked Alyx.

"That would be amber, *gintaras* in Lithuanian, found on the Baltic Sea shores, and considered the best variety of amber."

"I didn't get a chance to take a close look at the jewelry counter in your store," said Alyx. "Did you bring back some amber jewelry?"

The question startled him. He quickly regained his composure, letting Alyx know that she'd asked one too many questions. But it was too late to change the subject.

"So, what brings you to the neighborhood?" she said.

"I wanted to see you," he said simply. "I brought the coffee and cookies to entice you, hoping you'd ask me to stay and share."

"It looks like it worked."

She stood up slowly, "Will you excuse me a minute? I'll be right back."

I sensed the fear in her, and I meowed once, the pre-arranged signal for the felines to take their strategic places—Misty on the back of the couch, Pooky next to Steele and I had the floor.

Alyx kept a small, six-inch gun hidden among the towels in the bathroom and when she came out, the gun securely held behind her back, she said "Sorry, coffee has that effect on me."

"You can put the gun away, Alyx," he said. "You don't need it. I'm not a murderer."

Alyx brought the weapon forward and rested her hand on her lap, finger solid on the trigger.

"I don't know how you guessed," he said, then added, "Althea was my mother, but I didn't kill her."

"Your mother? Were you at her condominium before she was killed?"

He nodded. "But I didn't kill her!" he repeated, running his fingers through his hair.

Alyx did her best to remain calm. It was clear she didn't know what to believe and neither did I. "Tell me what happened," she demanded of Steele.

"I learned about my kidnapping when my mother— or the woman I thought was my mother—died last year. In a deathbed confession, she told me the truth. She had been employed as a domestic in Althea's house in Africa. She—that is the woman who I have called mother—was appalled at what she perceived was Althea's apparent neglect of me. She couldn't have any children, and when her husband approached her with an idea, she agreed to the kidnapping only if they could keep the baby. She and her husband had friends in the right places, and with their help, they got out of the country with me and the ransom money."

He paused. Alyx didn't ask any questions, and so he continued.

"We vacationed here in Beachside every year until I graduated from high school. I've always loved this area, and since my father was already living here, it made sense to open my business in the area as well. He actually found the location for me, and I pretty much did everything long-distance."

He took a sip of coffee, "I thought it a happy coincidence when I found out that Althea also lived in Beachside, thinking we could take our time to get to know one another as mother and son. However, she ignored the correspondence from the investigation firm that I'd hired to find her, and she refused to see me when I tried contacting her personally. On an impulse, I took a chance, believing that if I just showed up in person it would strike a motherly cord or something, so I went to see her and brought her a delicate necklace of amber beads. She was horrified to see me and when she opened the box that I forced on her, she immediately tried to pull the necklace apart, throwing it hard against the stairwell while she screamed at me to get out. I quickly picked up the necklace, put it back in the box and left. I was devastated. Later, I learned she was dead."

I wasn't sure I believed the man and everything he'd said—Althea screaming and throwing things against the wall didn't fit the character of the woman I knew. However, it was true that Althea hadn't told the whole truth about herself, had she?

"Have you tried to get in touch with your cousin, Carole Berth?" Alyx asked him.

He nodded, leaned back, and draped his arm across the back of the couch, invading Misty's space. She didn't budge, and he removed his arm.

"She refused to see me and told me not to call her again."

"Did you know that Althea was a wealthy woman?"

"Yes, I did," he sighed. "That gives me a solid motive, doesn't it? Except, I have plenty of my own money and I certainly wouldn't kill for more," he added emphatically, if not necessarily convincingly.

"I'm never surprised at what people will do for money," she said off-handedly.

For an instant, his eyes turned hard, and then he looked away.

"Were you angry at her when she refused to acknowledge you?" she asked.

"At first I was, but I knew about her illness, and that excused her behavior in my mind. I'm fine with it now. I have no feelings for her one-way or the other. I looked

for her believing it would ease her pain of not knowing
what had happened to her child, but apparently I
shouldn't have bothered."

"I think she blocked out your existence to protect
herself."

He said he was fine with it; but I heard something
different in his voice.

Alyx began in a soft tone, "I met Althea when she
came into the store last spring…"

She then told him all she knew about his real mother
up to the day that she'd found her body. Jonathan sat
quietly and listened. After that, they ran out of things to
say.

Alyx didn't put the gun away until Steele had left the
house. Then she securely locked the door behind him.

*"Independent as they are, cats find more than pleasure
in our company."*
—Lloyd Alexander

CHAPTER THIRTY-FIVE: *The Last Umatilla Trip*

Alyx didn't want to give Carole Berth the opportunity to say no, so she didn't call ahead before driving to Umatilla again. The temperature was in the high seventies and the sun was shining as usual. It was a lovely day and I was enjoying myself. Better known for palm trees, the beach and Walt Disney World, we drove through the part of Florida that most people from out of state don't know exists. We passed several miles of agricultural fields, a small grove of orange trees, and an open field with cattle grazing contently, some up close to the fence, their big brown eyes watching the occasional vehicle drive by.

We arrived at Carole's door before noon. A pale, sickly looking twenty-something young man answered the door. Alyx gave her name and asked to see Carole.

"She's not home," he wheezed.

"Do you know when she'll be back?"

"No clue," he shrugged.

"Do you mind if I sit out here and wait for a while?"

"Fine with me," he responded and he closed the door.

She came back to the car and we waited. At one point, I caught the movement of a curtain at one of the windows. I didn't think it was Carole's son; the figure I glimpsed before it moved away was much larger. I thought it was probably her husband, and I had a fleeting idea as to why he was hiding from Alyx.

Carole finally arrived home, and was naturally surprised to see Alyx, not to mention me.

"What are you doing out here? Didn't anyone come to the door?"

"Yes, a young man, who I assume is your son, answered the door, and I told him I'd sit out here and wait for you. He seemed to be having trouble catching his breath, and I didn't want to make him feel any more uncomfortable. Does he have heart problems?"

"No, he's full of allergies and has asthma. As you can guess, he doesn't spend much time outdoors. I'm sorry, did we have an appointment that I forgot?" she asked, more than a little annoyed, I thought.

Alyx pulled the check from the estate sale out of her bag and handed it to her.

"I thought since I had the time, I'd bring this to you."

Carole took the check and shoved it in her purse. "That really wasn't necessary, I told you it was all right to mail it," she said.

"Well, it's a little more than what I felt comfortable mailing. We sold almost everything and paid you for the items we kept. I'll arrange for those few things we didn't sell to be picked up this week if you don't mind me keeping the key a few days longer."

I looked hard for any reluctance and didn't see any— —only irritation.

"Actually, the truth for my visit is that I have some questions, and I hope you understand that I have to do whatever I can to help find Althea's killer."

"You still want to help her even though my aunt lied to you?"

"If, as you say, she was sick, then she wasn't responsible for her behavior."

Carole pursed her lips in resignation but still didn't invite us in. "So what do you want to know?"

"Detective Smarts isn't obligated to tell me anything, and he hasn't, even though I found two pieces of evidence that he missed. Judging from the contents of the lingerie chest that were scattered on Althea's bed, you must have been looking for something too. Did you find what you were looking for?"

"I really have to go. My husband is waiting for something he asked me to pick up for him."

Alyx stepped off the porch and abruptly turned around before Carole turned the knob.

"Does your husband have a heart condition?"

"I don't see how my family's health is of any concern to you. No, he doesn't."

That was the end of the conversation. She left Alyx standing there and went into the house without a backward look.

*"The sun rose slowly, like a fiery fur ball coughed up
uneasily onto a sky-blue carpet by a giant unseen cat."*
—Michael McGarel

CHAPTER THIRTY-SIX: *The Train Station Incident*

"Hi, Maggie, I know you were worried about my trip
to Umatilla, so I thought I'd let you know," Alyx said
into her cell phone as we wound our way back home.
"I'm on my way back, about twenty miles out, taking a
side trip to the Amtrak railroad station, mostly for
sentimental reasons."

She told Maggie that she remembered the time she'd
taken ten year-old Ethan on his first train ride—taking
the train to the next stop and back. She said that
according to the article she'd read in the paper, the
station, originally built in 1813, had a doubtful future as
there was only a small amount of money earmarked for
its rehab project.

The right exit came up; the route took us through an
older residential neighborhood to Old New York
Avenue, and into the empty, gravel parking lot of the
station. Alyx got out of the car and walked the short
distance to the benches on the boarding platform. She
seemed preoccupied as she walked slowly back to the
car, unaware of a vehicle until it swerved in front of
her. As the wheels spun on the gravel, the driver rolled
down his window and yelled, "Watch out, you stupid
woman!"

The car didn't touch her, but disoriented by the action, Alyx fell on her knees. A station employee ran towards her and helped her up.

"Are you all right?"

Alyx brushed off her knees. "Yes, I think so. Did you see what happened?"

"Yes, I did. That car drove in slowly and picked up speed when it swerved in front of you. It looked to me like he did it on purpose."

"Did you recognize the make of the car?" she asked.

"I'm sorry; I don't know one from the other, and I didn't even look at the tag. Do you want me to call the police?"

"No, there's not much I can tell them other than it was a black sedan. I didn't see the tag number either."

After the incident, we drove directly to the police station in Beachside. A tall, skinny man with a potbelly and a few strands of dirty hair was telling an officer at the front desk about an altercation with his neighbor, a two-inch cut on his cheek still fresh but not bleeding.

The officer wrote down all the information about the man's complaint on a form, and then took care of two people over the phone before he turned his attention to Alyx, thirty minutes later.

Busy filling out a log sheet, he didn't even look up when he asked if he could help her.

"Yes, ma'am. What can I do for you?"

She skipped the small talk that usually accompanied her requests. "I'd like to speak to Detective Smarts."

"He's not in the station at the moment, ma'am."

"He is on duty today?"

"Yes, he is."

"Is there any way you can reach him?"

He looked at his watch. "Are you sure no one else can help you?"

She bit her lower lip. "I received a threating note, and someone just tried to run me over. I prefer to speak to Smarts, but, yes, someone else can help me."

"Your name?"

"Alyx Hille and this involves the Althea Burns' case."

The officer looked up and smiled. After a discreet phone call, Detective Smarts appeared a few minutes later, a toothpick dangling from his mouth.

He scanned the note Alyx handed him, and the smirk on his face quickly disappeared. He made no comment about my presence, but asked her to follow him down the hall to an office no bigger than a closet. He slid behind the desk and asked her to have a seat in one of the two folding chairs facing him. I took up guard next to her. She told him everything. He listened without interruption.

"Is that all? You've told me everything?"

She nodded and looked down, her hand clasped tightly around my leash.

"Thank you, Ms. Hille. I know you don't think much of my detective skills, but I assure you, we've been working on the case. Although we didn't get any prints off the pill case you found, I did learn that Carole Berth's husband takes nitroglycerine for angina."

I wasn't surprised to hear that.

"Ms. Hille, as far as I'm concerned, this case is now a priority, and if anything else happens … call nine-one-one, then call me immediately." He pulled a business card from his pocket, "My cell phone number is on there."

We left the station. I was feeling assured and I hope Alyx was too. When we arrived at the shop, Maggie got up from the couch when we walked into the workroom, and stepped forward to unhook my leash. "It's about time you got back. I've been sitting here waiting and worrying," she scolded.

"I thought you had plans outside the store today," said Alyx.

"I did and I do. I expected you back sooner. What happened in Umatilla?"

Alyx closed the workroom door. "You were right to worry this time; someone tried to run me over at the train station. Actually, I think he was just trying to scare me," she began and she ended with the visit to the police station.

"You did the right thing talking to Detective Smarts. I think you should stay at my place or I can stay with you, if you'd rather not leave the cats alone."

"It's okay, Maggie. If the guy in the car had really wanted to kill me, he wouldn't have swerved to avoid me."

"What about the nitro case you found?"

"Smarts said Carole's husband takes nitroglycerine for angina, but there's no proof the case I found belonged to him. I know you're concerned, and it worried me too, but now that Smart knows everything, I think it will be okay."

Maggie gave her a hug. "Promise you won't go to Umatilla again."

"I can definitely promise you that I will not make the trip again."

"If you yell at a cat, you're the one who making a fool of yourself."
—Unknown

CHAPTER THIRTY-SEVEN: *An Apology of Sorts*

Jim Husen, an antiques dealer whom Alyx had met a couple of years earlier at a Miles-Long-Garage-Sale event on A1A, stopped in to see her. He said he had a customer who collected globes, and he wondered if she happened to have any or knew anyone who did.

"As a matter of fact, I do have a globe," she said, and directed him to the side of the store, near the staircase.

"It's been here since we opened. I don't know much about it, other than it's from the 1930s, produced by the George F. Cram Company in Indianapolis."

The globe she'd referred to was very decorative with Atlas holding up the globe between two columns.

"You know," said Jim, "some of these can go for real good money. I heard about a tiny 1790s pocket globe that sold for fifteen-thousand dollars."

I was impressed. Alyx's globe probably wasn't that valuable, but it still might draw nice sum. Of course, not all deals went that smoothly. Some dealers were greedier than others; they weren't satisfied with just making a profit. They wanted to squeeze every last penny they could out of the deal. I knew that as far as Alyx was concerned, that took the fun out of it.

Somehow, Antiques & Designs managed to prosper without gouging anyone in the process.

Alyx had another item sitting nearby that had not attracted any attention. It was a duck decoy. She asked Jim if he was interested, and told him all she knew about it.

"This and that globe were the first two items I purchased with the intent of selling them in my store someday," she told him. "Anyway, the Mason Decoy Company in Detroit, Michigan—my home state—produced three grades of decoys—premium, challenge, and standard. The standard typically featured glass eyes, and a hand-painted solid body. This is a standard decoy, made around 1910. The last time I'd checked, it was valued at fifteen hundred dollars. I'll negotiate if you find a buyer, and you'll get the ten percent dealer discount."

Jim picked up the decoy, turning it over in his hands to inspect it closer.

Suddenly, I felt her presence before I saw her. An elegantly dressed woman in a classic-style blue suit stood scrutinizing Alyx from top to bottom. She quickly looked away when Alyx turned in her direction.

"It looks like it's in excellent condition," said Jim about the decoy, "You should get full value for it. I'll mention it to some people."

"Great. Are you and Louise planning to go to the Williamsburg Antiques Forum in February?" Alyx asked him.

"We talked about it and think we might go. The theme this year is "The Arts of the American South" and that's right up my alley. My wife is looking forward to helping prepare an authentic eighteen-century dinner, and I'm looking forward to eating it. What about you?"

"Maggie and I talked about it, but at the time she wasn't interested. I love the place and its history and I don't need a reason to go."

"Well, if you decide to go, you're welcome to come with Brenda and me. You know our RV is big enough to handle more than the two of us."

She knew that to be true, as she and Maggie had gone on a trip with the Husens once before.

"Thanks, Jim. I'll keep it in mind. Tell Brenda I found that recipe she asked me for, and I'll give her a call soon."

Alyx completed the transaction, Jim left, and she turned her attention to the woman who introduced herself as David Hunter's ex-wife, Joann.

"David said I should apologize."

"You're here because David told you to? What are you making him do for this apology?"

"Nothing he doesn't want to do," she replied slyly.

"We'll see about that," Alyx said defiantly.

Joann's pale blue eyes flashed to her face, her full lips stretched thin. "You're not very gracious, are you? You're nothing but a garbage picker."

"Yes, that's what I do, and I hope to do more of it," replied Alyx. She made it abundantly clear that she wasn't willing to give David up that easily.

After the door closed behind Joann Hunter, Alyx literally dropped into the nearest chair. Wanting to comfort her, I jumped on her lap and accidentally knocked over a small picture with a decorative inlaid top sitting on the side table. Both the table and the picture had come from Althea's bedroom. Alyx had told Maggie that she kept the picture—a soft garden scene surrounded by a delicate gold frame—not so much for its value, but more because it reminded her of Althea.

The photo landed on its face, exposing a brown paper backing that had come unglued. Alyx picked it up and took it to the workroom, searched for glue to fix it. When she lifted the paper to re-glue it, something caught her eye—another photograph was behind the first—a smaller, black and white photograph of a young woman holding a baby.

Althea hadn't forgotten her son.

About an hour later, Hunter walked through the door. His presence commanded our attention. Misty came to stand next to me and wanted to know what was going on. Hunter surveyed the room slowly, and quickened his step when Alyx came into view on the other side of the store.

"Alyx, I need to speak to you in private for a moment."

"Did she come crying to you that I didn't graciously accept her apology?" Alyx asked him.

He looked at her blankly. "I don't know what you're referring to, but you'll want to hear what I have to tell you."

"Joann," said Alyx, "She came to apologize for harassing me. She said you told her she should."

She turned and walked away. David followed, dodging furniture and cats in trying to keep up with her.

"I told her no such thing."

Her dead stop caused a collision of cats, furniture, and humans.

He reached for her hand and she didn't pull away. "I realized what she was doing after I spoke to you. I told her that she and I were finished, that I was ready to move on and I hoped she'd do the same."

"Okay, then."

A non-committal answer for sure, but apparently the only one he was going to get.

"Now can I speak to you in private?" he reiterated.

She nodded, "Let's go to the workroom."

"I know you're seeing Jonathan Steele and there's something you need to know about him."

"How do you know that I've been seeing him?" she asked, rightfully suspicious. They sat at the table.

"How I know isn't important. What's important is what my source told me about him."

She wasn't listening anymore. "You've been following me?"

He didn't answer. "Listen, Alyx. Jonathan Steele is Althea's son."

She leaned back in her chair, daring him to tell her something she didn't know.

"I know that."

"Did he tell you that he doesn't have a penny to his name, and that he doesn't actually own the store, that it's owned by several people?"

Alyx was stunned. "The inventory is his, isn't it?"

He shook his head. "Most of it's on consignment from overseas distributors; very little is his."

"So what do you think this has to do with me?"

He stood and leaned over her desk. "I heard your store was broken into, and that only Althea's furniture was disturbed. Could he have been looking for another will—one that left everything to him? He could use the money, and I bet his cousin Carole Berth isn't willing to share."

"You think he killed Althea?"

"Alyx, I care about you. I wanted to warn you, to tell you to be careful; that's all."

"Thank you, David."

He left, and she sat at her desk, cradling her head.

"There are many cat quotes: some are clever, some are funny, and some are true, but a true ailurophile knows that we are as unique as any human."—Murfy

CHAPTER THIRTY-EIGHT: *A Problem With the Security System*

It was almost bedtime. The phone rang and at first, no one moved. Alyx answered on the second ring. "Sorry for the late call, Ms. Hille. I thought you'd want to know that there seems to be a problem with the alarm system at Antiques & Designs."

Alyx sat up, and I scooted closer. "What kind of problem?"

"The alarm is malfunctioning at its location. Would you like to have someone take a look at it tonight or wait until tomorrow?"

She hesitated for an instant. "I think you'd better send someone tonight."

"Alfred Simms is on call. He'll be driving his own vehicle rather than a company car and will meet you there in about fifteen minutes."

Alyx was still wearing the shorts and tee shirt she'd put on that morning. She slipped into a pair of sandals and quickly went out the door with me on her heels. We pulled up behind the shop and the second I saw the parked black sedan, I immediately recognized the heavy-set man waiting by the back door—the same man who'd tried to run her over at the train station.

Alyx parked in a lighted section of the parking lot. She opened the door, and I catapulted out of the truck. Hissing violently, I galloped ahead, and lunged at the man's head. He raised his arms to protect himself and knocked me flat against the brick wall. Alyx quickly got the picture, but instead of running away, she started running towards me. He pulled out a gun that was tucked in his waistline, fired a shot and missed. Alyx ducked behind a cement light pole five feet in front of her.

"It's your fault; you should have minded your own business. I tried to warn you but you ignored the note on the truck and you ignored what happened at the train station. Why didn't you leave it alone? The old bitch never did anything for anybody."

I recovered enough to creep behind him and plan my attack while he blubbered on. He almost sounded sorry when he said, "You should have stayed out of it. I have no choice. Now I have to kill you."

He took a step forward, and at that moment, I leaped up and sank my fangs deep into the fleshy part of his right leg, right above the ankle. He repeatedly tried to knock me off with his gun and missed for the most part, succeeding only in making me determined to hang on. The rest is a blur until Tim Schaumburg, a private investigator and a friend of David Hunter said, "Okay, Murfy, you can let go now; I have it."

I hate the taste of human flesh, and so I promptly let go. Tim didn't expect me to understand what he'd said, and, as it often happens, that look of amazement mixed with doubt appeared on his face. It was like catnip to me.

Alyx made a fuss over me while she checked for wounds, and held me gently, careful not to touch the tender spots.

"Thank you so much for your help, Tim. How did you happen to be here?"

"I'm not here by accident; David asked me to keep an eye on you."

"David Hunter asked you to do that?"

He nodded once. "I was watching your house, intending to leave when you went to bed—hoping it would be soon. When you drove away instead, I knew it meant trouble, and so I followed you. I called the police on the way, and I called David who's going to meet us at the police station."

"If a cat does something, we call it instinct; if we do the same thing, for the same reason, we call it intelligence."
—Will Cuppy

CHAPTER THIRTY-NINE: *The Cat Genius*

Alyx left with Hunter for a late breakfast. Trying to catch up on some of the sleep I'd missed, I lay flat on my back, feet up in the air in my favorite chair while my housemates paced the perimeter of the room, eager to discuss the events of the previous night. I reluctantly gave up my quest for sleep, stretched my sore body, and faced my inquisitors.

I explained that Carole Berth's husband, Michael, had confessed to killing Althea, and also to trying to kill Alyx, who'd been on the right track from the beginning.

Michael was having financial problems worse than his wife knew. He and his son went to Althea to ask for help, but she refused because she thought he'd tried to talk Carole into declaring her incompetent and put her away in a nursing home and take control of her money. His frustration led to rage and he killed her.

At first, Carole didn't know who killed Althea; the night of the murder, her husband and son were supposed to have gone to a basketball game. She became suspicious when Smarts questioned her about the pill case. Then, she questioned her son and he confessed that the pill case had broken off when his father was struggling with Althea. Carole and her son searched the condominium one last time before the estate sale. Her son was looking for the pill case, and Carole was looking for another will or codicil leaving the money to Althea's son, Jonathan, intending to destroy it, if she found it.

Michael never wanted to kill Alyx, but when she showed up in Umatilla asking leading questions, he knew that it was only a matter of time before she figured everything out. He followed her to the train station to convince her of the danger she faced.

He was also the one who broke-into the store in an effort to throw suspicion on Jonathan Steele. Michael Berth sells and installs security systems, so getting into the store was no problem. He intended to push the theory that Steele believed Althea had made another will, leaving everything to him and he was looking for that will.

Misty didn't consider that smart thinking on Michael's part, and she had a good point. How would Jonathan Steele know what furniture was Althea's anyway? The only answer I could give her was that desperate men don't think smart, and consequently do desperate things. In this case, however, all of Althea's things were marked 'Burns Estate' and mostly, all in one place, but no one knew that.

Pooky questioned how I knew that's what happened. I could have said that according to my mother, I'm not an ordinary tabby and the *M* on my forehead is the proof. A simpler truth is that I'm pretty good at processing information. Misty wondered if that meant I was a *genius cat.*

I don't know the answer to that question and that makes it an excellent question. I venture to say that all animals possess some level of intelligence—humans call it instinct. Some humans agree with my observation and they will probably one day design an IQ test that is not human-centric and appropriate for animals in scope and scale according to their species. Maybe then, the age-old question of who's more intelligent—a cat or a dog—now based on the number of words they recognize, will be forever settled.

In the small hours of the morning, I made my last trip to the abandoned shed. If Simon thought the group of about thirty cats would intimidate or persuade me to leave with them, he was wrong on both counts. I was right about his fake altruism—he was forming his own clowder, had heard about my tactical fighting prowess, and wanted me to help him conquer other clowders and territory.

I made it clear that I was living out my life with Alyx, to comfort her and protect her and those she loved, and, if possible, I intended to do it to the best of my ability.

Simon and I are bound to meet again someday, maybe under different circumstances. But that will probably be the last life for one of us.

THE END

ABOUT THE AUTHOR

 ANNA KERN grew up in East Pointe, Michigan, and lives in St. Johns County, Florida. Retirement allows her to enjoy every minute of her free time doing what she loves to do best— write. DEADLY DIAMOND is her second novel in the Murfy the Cat Mystery series and she is working on a third. A PAWS-IBLE THEORY is Murfy's first adventure. Visit Anna at https://www.facebook.com/anna.kern.author.

www.ingramcontent.com/pod-product-compliance
Lightning Source LLC
Chambersburg PA
CBHW020329260626
47156CB00004B/1447